Praise for Braking for Bodies…

A wonderfully entertaining mystery. Colorful and eclectic characters abound. The pace and storyline are perfect. The writing is descriptive and superb. The characters are well developed and always interesting. Author Duffy Brown writes with such panache and humor. the *Open Book Society*

The dialogue is great, the setting beautiful, and the characters ever-changing. I look forward to more adventures with Evie. *King's River Life magazine*

As with every *Duffy* Brown book she has a way of weaving humor into her mystery and this one doesn't disappoint I found myself laughing out loud more than once

Community Bookstop

The story grabbed my attention from the very beginning and held it all the way through to the end of the story. I can hardly wait for the next adventure on the island!

Book Babble

An absolutely enjoyable romp on Mackinac Island. I heartily recommend this book to anyone looking for a light-hearted, amusing, cozy mystery. *Give Me A Book*

Duffy Brown just seems to get better with each book she writes. Braking for Bodies is filled with humor and the mystery is laced with first-rate misdirection. *Kittling Books*

a great, fun mystery with great characters and an excellent setting. The perfect recipe for a great cozy mystery series. *Books Are Life*

The characters in this book were enjoyable and the setting very quaint. The author did a good job of giving you just enough so you thought you had it figured out but then realize you do not. *A Holland Reads*

Books by Duffy Brown

Consignment Shop Mysteries

Iced Chiffon

Killer in Crinolines

Pearls and Poison

Dead Man Walker

Demise in Denim

Lethal in Old Lace

Cycle Path Mysteries

Geared for the Grave

Braking for Bodies

Tandem Demise

Tandem Demise

Duffy Brown

Edition: November 2018

Hi, everyone and welcome back to Mackinac Island and life with no cars and only horses, bikes and foot-power to get around. Fall is in full swing with the leaves changing colors, a chill in the air and gardens ablaze with mums of every hue.

I love this island that is part of Michigan and located where Lake Michigan meets Lake Huron. Life on Mackinac moves a bit slower with cell phone service not all that reliable and internet not all that important. Why look at a screen when you can a take bike ride to the Grand Hotel for high tea or visit Fort Mackinac for a musket drill or firing a cannon.

The only way to get to Mackinac is by ferry. Taxis here are horse drawn affairs moving at about five miles an hour and riding bikes is a breeze with no horns honking or traffic to maneuver around. This is an island for getting away, for relaxing, for enjoying life with friends and family. It's life the way it used to be. Once you visit Mackinac Island a piece of you will forever stay there and you will long to return.

I visited the island with my daughter from NCY. She went from Times Square and a hectic design job to no cars or cell service within twenty-four hours. When we got off the ferry she said, "Do you think we died and went to heaven?"

I've used all the real streets, restaurants, bars, hotels, piers, and ferry lines. I've included names of proprietors of the bookstore, bars, inns and markets. My characters order off the actual menu in the restaurants, drink at the watering hole where the locals meet and have the same problems with tourists...called fudgies...that the islanders have. I made the Cycle Path mysteries real so when you visit the island you will feel as if you've already been there. That you are coming home.

Happy reading and I hope you fall in love with Mackinac Island and that you have as much fun with *Tandem Demise* as I did writing it.

Hugs,

Duffy

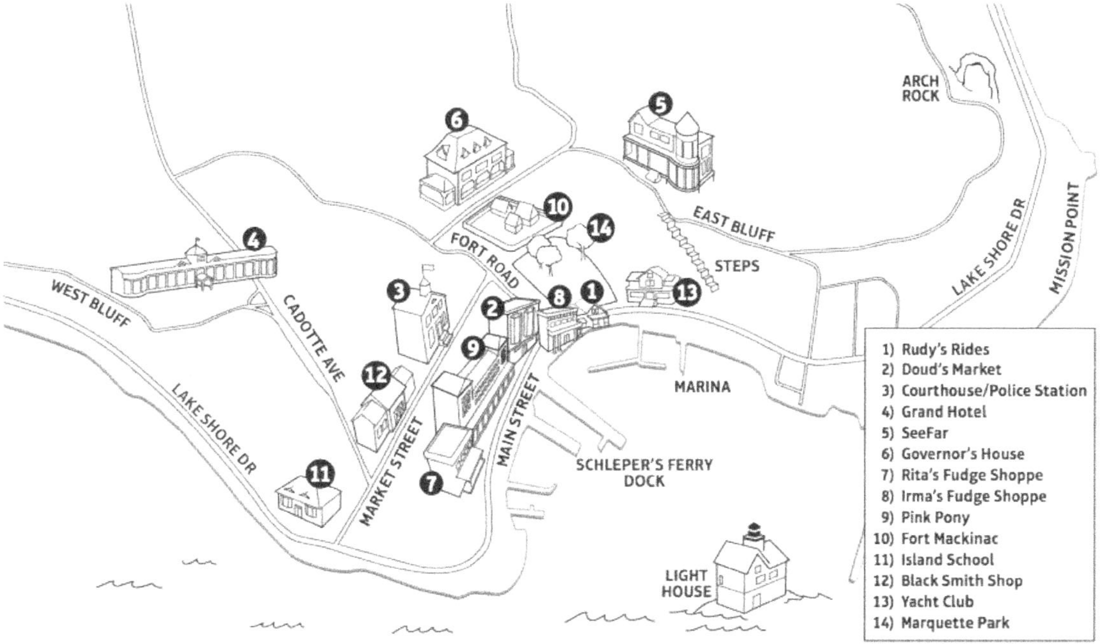
ARCH ROCK
MISSION POINT
LAKE SHORE DR
EAST BLUFF
STEPS
FORT ROAD
WEST BLUFF
CADOTTE AVE
MARKET STREET
MAIN STREET
MARINA
SCHLEPER'S FERRY DOCK
LIGHT HOUSE
LAKE SHORE DR
1) Rudy's Rides
2) Doud's Market
3) Courthouse/Police Station
4) Grand Hotel
5) SeeFar
6) Governor's House
7) Rita's Fudge Shoppe
8) Irma's Fudge Shoppe
9) Pink Pony
10) Fort Mackinac
11) Island School
12) Black Smith Shop
13) Yacht Club
14) Marquette Park

Chapter One

"Do you think he's dead or just dead drunk?" I asked Fiona as the two of us stood alone on the freight dock with thick night fog swirling around us. We were staring at a guy prone on the pier with a champagne bottle clutched in his arms.

I grabbed Fiona's hand as we shuffled a little closer. "Uh oh, he's staring back at us and not in a *Hey come have a drink with me* kind of way."

"And there's blood, a lot of blood." Both of us shivered, from the wind gusts off Lake Huron as much as from our present situation.

"This is terrible." Fiona made the sign of the cross and I did the same. I wasn't Catholic, but I needed to do something and right now there weren't a lot of options. "How does this keep happening to you?"

I did a double-blink and stared at Fiona. "Excuse me?"

"Mackinac's a little island and you're here tonight picking up kites to sell at your bike shop but instead - oh gee guess what - you come across yet another body!"

"Hold on a minute - stop right there." I dropped Fiona's hand and jabbed her on the forehead partially covered by the purple sequin paperboy cap befitting her occupation of *Town Crier* editor. "Forget the *you* part about the bodies. Okay, the first one was mine - I'll give you that - but the last one was definitely a *we* body. *We* both found it and you're the one who was accused of making it dead and this is not my fault."

"All I know is when you landed here two years ago, Irish Donna said there was a black cloud hanging over you. If this corpse is any indication, the cloud hasn't changed one bit. I think it's getting darker."

"Maybe a little." I took a closer look at the body as the waves lapped at the shoreline and wood pilings under our feet. "Do you recognize him?"

"No, but he's cute." Fiona's words mixed with the foghorn bellowing in the harbor, her breath making little puffy moisture clouds that faded into the night. "Well, he was cute when he didn't have that big gash on the side of his head and don't give me that *how can you say such a thing* look, Evie Bloomfield. I lived in LA for three and two-thirds years and covered some pretty grizzly stuff. Maybe he's from one of the work ferries or barges. This is the island's freight dock and he's dressed in jeans and a work jacket."

"The most grizzly thing you ever did out in LA was chow down on bad TexMex. You were a rag reporter covering celeb affairs, scandals, and the occasional *I had Elvis's baby*."

"Why couldn't you just pay for delivery like everyone else does on this island?" Fiona huffed. "Then Captain wouldn't have to hide the boxes of kites for you to pick up tonight and I wouldn't be mixed up in something I can't even put in the *Crier*. One whiff of a body around here and tourists will run for the ferries, taking their American Express cards with them and turning this island into a ghost town. Dead guy on dock is not a great tourist attraction."

I was a *come-here* to Mackinac Island and Fiona was a *born-here*. In the last two years we'd bonded over OPI nail polish, Nutty Buddy ice cream cones, and a knack for snooping that included picking locks and telling whopper lies with a straight face. In my other life back in Chicago I'd been a grunt-level graphic designer. I wound up on the island when I tried to suck up to my boss to land a promotion. My great plan was to help her father who owned a bicycle shop and had broken his leg. That he got nailed for a murder on my watch did not help my promotion chances. I now owned part of Rudy's Rides and painted old, rusted bikes shiny new again with such themes as golf, Batman, Babe Ruth - the baseball player and candy bar - or any other love-of-your-life you'd like to sport around town.

Fiona, who had felt the need to spread her wings, took a second-rate rag reporter job in LA and got accused of killing her boss when he followed her back to Mackinac. Not all homecomings were *Welcome Home* banners, brass bands, and family cookouts.

"What we should do," Fiona offered, "is not touch anything and call the police, except Molly's on desk duty tonight and you know how she is with bodies. Nate's usually hanging around, but he's up at the Grand Hotel at a hundred-bucks-a-plate dinner getting an award for spearheading the campaign to repair the limestone walls around Fort Mackinac. After two hundred fifty years they're starting to look like Swiss cheese. Sutter's having his dessert about now and raspberry crème brûlée is his fave. He won't be happy if we drag him away."

"Happy? Well I'm sure as heck not happy keeping company with a dead guy and you don't look too happy and Mr. Champagne is staring up at the sky and doesn't have a smile on his face either, so that makes it Nate's turn. He's the chief of police around here and gets paid for not being happy. I'm ringing him up."

"You're just pissed that you didn't get crème brûlée."

I dug Sheldon, my beloved iPhone with *Penny, knock, knock, knock* as a ring tone, out of my jacket pocket and held it to the sky. This was more a valiant effort of looking for service bars than actually expecting to find any.

Mackinac Island was known for many things like big horses; lots of bikes; the Grand Hotel that was truly grand; festivals for jazz, lilacs, ponies and selling ten tons of fudge a year to the tourists we lovingly called fudgies. Mackinac Island was not known for great cell phone service. Heck, it was known for *no* cell phone service.

“Surprise, surprise. No bars,” Fiona said looking over my shoulder. I pocketed the phone I used for playing Candy Crush and taking selfies. The foghorn moaned again, mixing with the deep rumble of a passing freighter somewhere out there in the pea soup.

“Well, we can’t just leave the body. What if the killer comes back for it,” I finally said, trying to come up with a plan.

“Or comes back and gets us.” We eyed the string of hazy fluorescents dotting the pier and leading back to the warehouse where we started. “You know it’s locked.”

“There’s a landline inside and these are desperate times.” We trudged our way back up the pier, gravel crunching beneath our feet, as we crossed the lane to the warehouse. Byline, Fiona's horse, whinnied and pawed the ground, telling us he was tired of pulling a cart all day and wanted to go home to a nice barn and fresh hay. I could relate, except for the barn and hay part. I was more of a flannel Hello Kitty nightshirt and hot cocoa kind of girl.

"This rock should work." I picked it up and started toward the warehouse window when Fiona grabbed my hand. "What in the world are you doing? Captain will have a canary if you bust a window. Just pick the freaking lock. That zipper pull on your fleece has two purple paperclips attached. My guess is they're not strictly for decoration and if you break the window, it'll set off an alarm."

"Nate can contact the alarm company to shut it off and if I pick the lock, he'll get suspicious about other conveniently opened doors during our island capers. The rock is an innocent bystander, same as me."

"Girlfriend, when it comes to you, Nate will never believe the innocent part."

Twenty minutes later Nate Sutter, local police chief and celebrated hunk, trotted toward us on Shakespeare, his trusted steed. Through the mist I could barely make out *Police* stenciled in reflector yellow across his windbreaker and baseball cap. “What, no tux?”

“Shakespeare’s got a phobia about bowties.” Sutter studied Fiona then me then the busted window. “Captain’s going blow a gasket. Why didn’t you just pick the lock?”

“Told you so,” Fiona sing-songed as Nate slid to the ground. “How was the benefit?”

“Irish Donna ate my crème brûlée and I got a flintlock pistol to hang on my wall. I would have rather had my crème brûlée.” Sutter tied Shakespeare to a post by the bike rack, Mackinac’s version of a parking lot. He unstrapped a black pouch from the saddle before following Fiona and me onto the dock, our footsteps making hollow sounds against the wood planks. Another forlorn foghorn blast reverberated through the darkness, the sound chilling me to my bones. If that headless horseman guy had galloped past us I wouldn’t have been one bit surprised. Actually, I would have peed my pants, but I’m just saying he would have fit right in.

"There." I nodded to the body. "Poor guy. He didn't deserve this."

Sutter's steps slowed before he stopped dead. His jaw tightened, his hands in a fist. What was that all about? He slowly pulled a camera from the pouch and snapped away, the flashes blindingly bright against the darkness. He moved side to side for different angles then hunkered down beside the body cocooned in the damp mist.

"Why didn't the killer just dump the body in the water?" I added. "I mean, why leave it out here on the dock for the entire world to see. We've got two deep lakes right here - big ones. Disposing of a body is a snap."

There was no response from Sutter, who usually recited a litany of police platitudes in these situations. *Don't touch anything, stay out of my way,* and - my personal favorite- *this is police business so get lost*. Like that means anything to two self-proclaimed busybodies. Fiona and I exchanged *what's going on* looks and I waved my hand in front of the camera. "Yoo-hoo. Anybody home? Got any idea what's happened here, Mr. Police Officer?"

"How the heck should I know?" Sutter blurted a little too quickly. "And why don't you pay for delivery like everyone else does instead of fumbling around in the dark."

"Amen to that," Fiona grunted.

"Well," I pushed on, trying to connect the dots since Sutter was off in LaLa Land and Fiona was no help at all, griping at me about being cheap. "There aren't any freighters tied up to the docks tonight, so Captain and the workers probably knocked off at six or so. It gets dark around 7:30 and it's almost nine now. My guess is this happened in the last hour and a half when no one was around. A meeting of some kind? A celebration, since we got the champagne thing going on? But unless he's with Greenpeace, there are better places to party than around crates of recyclables."

Sutter didn't say a word and took a few more pictures before grabbing a flashlight from his jacket pocket. He pulled on plastic gloves and unfolded bags marked *Evidence*. He checked the guy's jean pockets, pulling out a pair of well-worn work gloves, a silver dollar money clip with a few bucks, a beat-up wallet, and a pocketknife with a wood handle. He opened the wallet and found John Bernard's driver's license, credit card, and insurance info plus a bent photo of a ponytailed guy in a white blazer with sexy scruff standing next to a limo.

"With money and credit cards, we can rule out theft as a motive," I said, "and look." I snagging Sutter's arm before he dropped the money clip in an evidence bag. "There's an inscription on the back." I pushed the flashlight closer and read, "*Best Man* and there's a date. There's writing on the knife too. *Groomsman* and another date."

Still not saying a word, Sutter removed a silver flask from the guy's jacket pocket.

"Flip it over," Fiona said to Sutter. "These aren't exactly typical dockhand acquisitions. I bet they're gifts from being in weddings. I see them in bridal magazines all the time." Fiona cut her eyes from me to Sutter, both of us staring at her. "Hey. I drool over the cakes, okay? Fewer calories and ... Look right there!" Fiona pointed to the flask. "It says *Best Man* and there's another date."

Fiona put her hand to her heart and sighed deeply. “He was one of the good guys and a friend to a lot of people who wanted him to be a part of the most important day of their lives. He’s like one of those dreamy guys on The Hallmark Channel. Why can’t I meet guys like this?”

“Dead ones?” Sutter groused.

“The men I meet are after one thing, sports and beer.”

“That’s two things.”

“Seems like one.”

“And he has a watch,” I added. “It’s a nice one. Well, it was. I bet that’s from being in a wedding too, probably a best man.”

Sutter unbuckled the watch and flipped it over. I leaned closer and read, *“Today, my husband. Forever, my best friend.”*

“He’s married!” Fiona sobbed, grabbing my hand as a light rain started to fall.

“Or he stole all this stuff,” said Sutter.

"You are such a cynic." I wiped away a tear.

"I'm a cop and a realist, something that you don't find on The Hallmark Channel." Sutter held the dead guy's arm, probably checking for stiffness. I was no forensic guru, but how stiff a stiff is tells a lot about the time of death.

"The killer was probably hiding and whacked John over the head with..." I looked around. "Something hard and narrow. There's a lot of recycling stuff to choose from and..." I snagged Sutter's hand that held the flashlight and aimed the light onto the wood dock. "Look, blood drops, but we're losing them in the rain." I followed the dots with the light. "They lead over there to the edge of the pier."

"Meaning the murder weapon's in the drink. Probably halfway to Canada by now along with his cell phone since we didn't find that either."

Sutter picked something up off the dock that was tucked under a recycling bin, its blade catching the light.

"Box cutter?" I said.

"And it's not inscribed," Sutter muttered.

"Our guy was expecting trouble if he had his box cutter out."

"Our guy?" Sutter gave me a *good grief* look.

"And it was under the recycling crate. Maybe the killer thought he tossed it in the lake with the murder weapon? It's hard to see in all this fog."

Not answering again, Sutter put the box cutter in a bag and sealed it, preserving any DNA evidence. Scary how much I knew about crime scenes these days. Sutter snapped pictures of the dock and blood drops then held his hand out to me. "Give me your jacket."

"The man's dead, Sherlock. There's no warming him up now."

Sutter stood. He turned slowly and offered a half smile. His body relaxed and he had a devilish glint in his eyes. The old Sutter was back. "Cute."

"Just wanted to see if you were paying attention."

"I'm always paying attention, Chicago. I'll wrap the champagne in an evidence bag and then with your jacket so we don't break it or screw up the fingerprints. I'll put my jacket on this guy to protect the evidence. Doc's due back from St. Ignace tomorrow and we can't just leave the body lying here as a photo op for tourists biking the island. The dock's covered in footprints and shrapnel from loading and unloading and the weather's getting worse by the minute. Forensic anything is impossible. We'll need to keep this quiet. I'll take the body in the carriage to the medical center and put it in the cooler, you two take Shakespeare, and about why not dump the body off the pier..."

Sutter draped his arm over my shoulder and brought me close. "Bodies float, Chicago. They get washed ashore with the tides, especially with the big diesels churning up the water. Disposing of a body has to be done right. They have to be tied and weighed down and dumped out in the middle of the lake. Something to keep in mind the next time you and your sidekick here think about dragging me away from dessert. I can take care of things from here. You two take care of my horse, then get back to whatever you were doing."

Before I could protest Sutter headed for the carriage, leaving Fiona and me alone on the dock. She zipped her fleece against the damp chill and pursed her lips. “Does Nate really think we’re going to let this dead guy on the docks thing go? We found him and like it or not your black cloud affliction might have something to do with the guy being dead.” She poked my forehead. “You owe him.”

“*We* owe him, but for right now we have other problems. First, we have to help Nate load up a dead body. Not my favorite pastime. Then...” I patted Shakespeare and handed Fiona the reins. “I sure hope you know how to drive this thing ‘cause I don’t have a clue.”

Chapter Two

"Hide me quick!" came a voice from below.

I teetered on the ladder while fastening a display kite to the ceiling of my bike shop... Well, Rudy's Rides was half my shop. I looked down at the thirty-something guy standing beside the cluttered workbench that also served as my cluttered desk. He wore a wrinkled blue shirt and a tie in worse shape, with sweat dotting his forehead. He was a bit Jude Law, a bit James Franco, and a whole lot drop-dead gorgeous. For the first time all day I forgot about the poor dead guy on the dock and Sutter being totally grouchy and wished I'd combed my hair.

"She's going to kill me."

"This is Mackinac, we don't get a lot of that." *If you disregard last night's adventures on the dock.* Since I didn't need to add to the present body count I said, "What can I do to prevent this unfortunate-?"

"Where is that good-for-nothing rat fink!" boomed a voice outside the shop. A woman ran past the front windows of the bike shop, her footsteps clattering across the wooden porch and her white veil streaming behind her.

"Please?" Delicious gave me a desperate, totally charming look.

"I don't care how dreamy Bladen Powers is or thinks he is, I'm going to wring his neck with my own two hands," came more of the ear-piercing shriek that sent chills down my spine.

Cleveland and Bambino hissed and dove under the pool table that sat in the middle of the bike shop. I pointed to the door at the back of the shop and said to Delish, who I assumed was Bladen, "Run!"

He flashed a smile that had me teetering on the ladder again then dodged around the line of bikes waiting to be rented out. He closed the door to the kitchen just as Wild Woman banged open the front door. Panting, she swiped wedding veil tulle from her face, stomped her foot, and jabbed her bouquet of wilted lilies at me.

"I know Bladen's here." Her beady eyes darted from one corner of the shop, bedecked with vintage bike posters, to the other. "He was supposed to rent bride and groom bikes so Cuddle Cakes and I could pedal to our rehearsal dinner tomorrow night and ride down Fort Street after our wedding reception. It was Bladen's idea. '*This will be great for pictures, Daniela,*' he said. '*Just think of your dress streaming out behind you like a Roman goddess,*' he said."

Daniela fluffed her veil, looking wistful for a second before the scowl returned. "But then that stupid police chief Stutter or Smutter or whatever won't give me a road variance to close down Fort Street so we can get the best pictures. And that's not all. Bladen and that wimpy assistant of his were supposed to check with the caterer and the choir at St. Ann's to make sure everything was ready and none of that is done! What kind of wedding planner does that?"

She spun around, but instead of leaving like I hoped she would, she pointed to *Bride* scripted in pink sequins across the back of her white fleece sweatshirt. "That's me! This is my wedding week, my time to be diva divine and not worry about details. Bladen said he'd take care of everything and so far the only thing he's taken care of is how much gel to put in his hair...though he does have really great hair. But what matters now is that I'm getting married up there at the Mackinac Fort in two days... Two!"

"At a reenactment?"

"Do I look like I'm going to a reenactment! I'm a bride, a real one. Not just anyone can get married at the fort, only people who count. My three-times great-grandfather was Daniel Robertson, a Revolutionary War hero and commander of the fort. He counts and I, Daniela Robertson Smithfield, count and the Governor said I can have my wedding at the fort when nobody else can and I want Bladen Palmer's head on a platter right this minute!"

"I think it's called Fort Mackinac and is the platter for after you strangle Bladen?"

That got me an *eat dirt and die* look. I tied a knot in the string to secure the yellow and blue striped kite to the rafters and climbed down the ladder. "The problem is," I offered in my best *mommy to screaming two-year-old* voice, "I've already rented the bride and groom bikes but—"

"You what!" Daniela's face blotched red and her nostrils flared giving her a pug nose that would have looked great on a little piggy, not so much on a bride-to-be. "Where is Bladen?!"

Behind her back, Bladen stuck his head out the door, his blue eyes huge with a touch of charming desperation. I had never mastered charming, but I could relate to the desperation part. I'd been there a time or two, though with me it was more Midwest girl caught between a rock and bigger rock.

"How about I paint up two more bikes," I offered. I knew what it was like to have a messed up wedding and it wasn't fun. "I can have Bride and Groom bikes done by the day after tomorrow." Thanks to Red Bull and 5-Hour Energy. "I'll put a tux, top hat, champagne glasses, rings, and garter on one and a veil, flowers, cake, pearls, and lace on the other. We have so many weddings on the island I've been meaning to paint up another set of wedding bikes and you and Cuddle Bear—"

"Cuddle Cakes."

"Cuddle Cakes can ride down the Fort Street hill and get your great wedding pictures. A few people make the photos look more natural."

"I don't want natural, I want perfection." Daniela gave another swipe to her veil. "And I want a discount."

"Uh, I'm doing you a favor here."

"Bladen gets me discounts on everything, got me a great deal on the liquor. That and his hair and smile - he really has a sexy smile - are the reasons why I hired him in the first place. This wedding is costing me a fortune."

"I can do a discount." By overcharging, adding the discount, and ending up at the regular rate in the end. Whatever makes the customer happy.

Daniela snagged an orange Post-It pad off the workbench. "The wedding party's staying at Cedarhill on the East Bluff and here's the landline number if you need to reach me since cell phone service here is a joke. I swear the only bars around here are the drinking kind." Daniela tore off the top sheet and stuck the sticky note to the middle of my forehead, making my eyes cross.

"No wonder nothing gets done in this place!" she added. "Have the bikes up at the fort in time for the wedding and if you see that weasel Bladen or that mousy assistant of his tell them to pull some strings and get Fort Street closed for my pictures. Everything better be done right or else and I'm not kidding about the *or else*." Daniela snarled and stomped out of the shop, the door slamming behind her.

"You saved me." Bladen batted his long lashes as he came from the back of the shop. "My head might really be on that platter right now if you hadn't stepped in."

I peeled the Post-It from my forehead and stuck it to a can of chili-red paint that had other Post-Its on it and was sitting in the middle of my messy workbench. “Daniela had her heart set on the bikes.”

“You know brides. They overreact.”

“I don’t think you’ve got a prayer of getting Fort Street closed, but you probably should finalize arrangements with the chair and table rental people? You got the cake, right?”

Bladen added a sheepish grin. “I’m thinking cupcakes. I’ll get Petula, my PA, to whip up a batch.”

“You whip up brownies, not a wedding cake.”

“Cupcakes are in. Hey, I’ve got the booze covered,” he went on. “That’s what really matters at a wedding, right? Having top shelf liquor? I was doing weddings in Detroit and Wedding Wonderland transferred me here to set things up at this end. I’ve been a little busy.”

The liquor comment got my attention. “Liquor as in champagne?”

“With all the weddings I handle I get a lot of it shipped here in bulk at the best rates and I pick the cases up at the docks. Can't have good champagne and wine sitting in the hot sun. I have a barn to store supplies and ... What's with the twenty questions? You getting married?"

"Been there, done that. And crashed and burned. I was wondering about ... about delivery charges," I lied since I was fishing for information about John Bernard and his champagne bottle and getting nowhere. "I have freight shipped in and the charges really add up."

"It doesn't really matter to me. All that's included in the wedding fee." Bladen checked his watch. "I've got an engagement dinner party at the Metivier Inn down the street and need to check on the future bride." He added a wink. "That one's kept me real busy and has some nice perks." He laughed and was out the door, nearly colliding with Fiona carrying in a stack of newspapers.

She stopped, ogled, and stuck out her tongue and panted. "Holy wow, let me guess. Bladen Powers? I've heard the talk and I got to say that the visual does not disappoint."

I picked up a Hello Kitty kite from the lower side of the workbench and untied the Hello Kitty ribbon that held it together for shipping. “He’s like my ex. Talks a mean game, but actually has no game other than the World Series game where my ex happened to be instead of at the church marrying me.”

“Girl, he did you a favor and you know it.”

“Mother did me the favor. She bought the tickets to get rid of the ignoramus. That was her fancy term of endearment for him.”

“In the newspaper world we just go straight to jackass.” Fiona dropped a stack of *Town Criers* on the workbench and handed me a box she’d balanced on top. “Nate’s award that he left at the Grand. I dropped off papers and they asked me to give it to him, but I’m giving it to you. The glass lid’s loose so be careful it doesn’t slide off and break and this is your excuse to talk to Nate and wheedle info about our dead guy. Pretty clever, huh?”

“I rent bikes. You’re the reporter, you wheedle.”

"I'm more of a cut the crap and give me the facts kind of gal and Nate's never going to go for that. Besides I hate guns. You're the one from Chicago."

"FYI, island girl, not everyone in Chicago carries firearms."

"For Pete's sake," Captain grumped as he stomped into the shop, "it's the Good Soldier Award, a replica of an 1812 flintlock used here during that particular war of the same name and it's even got his initials on the handle. I'm sure Nate's mighty proud to get it, and it'll look great on his office wall."

"He would have rather had crème brûlée," Fiona mumbled then added in a louder voice, "Hi, Captain. How's it goin'."

Captain was unkempt and unshaven as usual. He wore his forever mangled seaman's cap and had his forever cigar dangling from the corner of his mouth, except this time it wasn't lit.

"Don't you 'Hi, Captain' me." As if by magic, the cigar didn't budge. He glared at Fiona then took the cigar from his lips and jabbed it in my direction. “Is there some reason you couldn’t just pick the blasted lock instead of busting my dang window last night? Now my insurance company’s on the warpath about me rewiring the whole warehouse with some bells and whistles alarm system to bring it up to snuff.”

“Me? Pick a lock?” I tried to look horrified.

Captain harrumphed. “Everyone knows you and Lois Lane here are always sticking your noses in everyone’s business and now it’s costing me personal.”

“Hey, our nose sticking solved two murders on this island without ruffling tourist feathers.” Fiona hitched her hip onto the lower workbench and Cleveland jumped into her lap, purring his head off. “The fudgies had no idea what was going on with those two murders and we didn’t lose one iota of business around here the whole summer. You should be thanking us. So, did you know the dead guy or what?”

“And why should I be telling you?”

“'Cause gossip's an Olympic sport on this island, right now you got the gold medal and we got to solve this murder fast and avoid a fudgie exodus.”

“Since you put it that way and appealing to my better business sense. The dead guy was a deckhand on the *Barefoot Gal*, one of the cargo ferries delivering goods. I knew him in passing, is all. He liked the island. Came back even when he wasn't docked here to spend time and grab a brew.”

“Didn't the *Barefoot Gal* realize all their crew wasn't onboard when they left port?” I asked.

Captain jabbed the cigar back in his mouth and struck a match. “My daughter's harping on me like a fishwife to quit smoking these things. Dang it all anyway.” He blew out the match. “Crews come and go, missy. They find a sweetheart, get to fighting, go gambling, and land in jail. When the ship leaves it shoves off no matter who's on board. Now about my window - who's gonna pay for that?”

Fiona sported a sassy grin. "The same guy who pays his workers under the table when putting in overtime and probably needs a new security system anyway."

Captain gave a shrug. "You got me this time. Can't blame a guy for tryin'."

He turned to go and I shoved the Hello Kitty kite in his hand. "For that new granddaughter. So, did Sutter know the guy on the dock?"

Captain held up the kite. "A bribe?"

"Kids love kites and these new special ones do dips and dives and Sutter's holding something back and I can't figure out why."

"More like you two can't tolerate being out of the loop and it's driving you crazy?"

"There is that."

Chapter Three

Captain glanced at the kite tucked under his arm. “Well, since you’re asking nice and adding presents. The only thing I picked up on was Nate calling the guy Larry and we all knew him as John Bernard. Guess Nate thought he recognized him, but didn’t after all?” Captain took the cigar from his lips, giving it a long look. “Ya’ know, these things were my best friend, gave me pleasure, and didn’t ask a darn thing in return.”

“Best friends don’t sneak up on you and kill you.”

“Ya got a point there.” Captain tossed the cigar in the trash then sauntered out the door.

“So, what do you think?” I asked Fiona.

“I think we should send Captain’s daughter a Thank You card for making him give up those smelly cigars.” She scooted off the workbench and set Cleveland on the pool table beside a sleeping Bambino. “And I think I got to get the rest of the *Criers* delivered around town and you got a note taped to a paint can saying Nancy Drew needs to be delivered to the Metivier Inn by five. It's five after, girlfriend, and for all our sakes, please tell me you're not riding that bike to the inn to deliver it. It's rush hour."

"We have big horses, slow bikes, and rush hour doesn't exist here. So what do you think about Sutter calling John Larry? Sutter doesn't make mistakes like that and last night Sutter was... weird. He was quiet and he's never quiet, especially when you and I are poking around his crime scene. It's like his brain was somewhere else. There's more here than mistaken identity, I can feel it in my bones."

"Winter's coming, that's what's wrong with your bones. They don't like the cold."

I grabbed a Batman kite from the box Fiona and I got from the pier last night, untied the ribbon holding it together, shook out the folds to unfurl the kite, and started up the ladder. "Calling Mackinac Island winters cold is like calling the Hope Diamond a bauble."

"You're a little old sissy pants from tropical Chicago and sometimes mistaken identity is just mistaken identity. Nate said he didn't know the guy, so why would he lie about it?

"And that is definitely the sixty-four dollar question of the day. The locals got the 4-1-1 on the dead guy the minute I smashed that warehouse window. So..."

"So you want me to ask around when I deliver the papers?" Fiona tipped me her sequin hat and headed for the door. "And for the low, low price of one beer at the Stang tonight I might even share the info. And you really need to straighten up this workbench."

"Then I'll never find anything."

"Don't forget about the glass lid and the wheedling."

Fiona closed the door behind her and I suspended Batman from the rafters and thought about Sutter. He recognized the guy on the dock, I could tell. So why not say so? What was the big deal? What was he hiding and he was definitely hiding something. I added a sunflower kite to the ceiling display then stored the ladder, stuffed the box of kites under the workbench, and tied the glass award box together with the Hello Kitty ribbon now smeared with bike grease. Yeah, I really did need to clean up the workbench.

I wound my way through the labyrinth of bikes to Nancy Drew. She was a red and black bike with the old grandfather clock on the back, the hidden staircase on the front, and a wicker basket with a magnifying glass strapped to the handlebars. I toed up the kickstand and grabbed my yellow fleece jacket.

"Don't give me that look," I said to Bambino and Cleveland, who were glaring at me from the middle of the pool table that took up residence in the bike shop each summer. In the winter the table literally got paraded back to the Mustang Lounge, aka the Stang, so the five-hundred locals braving the winters here of minus twenty and beyond could play, drink beer, and swap crazy tourist stories.

"I'm not riding this thing," I went on to the kits. "Just delivering it and I *am* getting better at staying upright, no matter what you think." I shoved up my sleeve and jutted my elbow. "See, the scab's nearly healed and the one on my knee is better and two years is not that long to learn how to ride a bike, so give me a break already."

Not looking one bit convinced, the disapproving duo went back to sleep as I pushed Nancy toward the door. I flipped the cardboard sign on the door from *Open* to *Closed* and arranged the hands on the little cardboard clock thing to the twelve and the six indicating I'd be back then. Not that there would be much bike renting at that hour, but there would be bike returns and when I got back I could start on the bride and groom bikes. I locked the door and headed down Main Street.

Twinkle lights already brightened the trees lining the street, highlighting the fact that the days were getting shorter and the nights longer. There were several customers in the Good Stuff Fudge Shop next to the bike shop. I waved to Rudy through the big plate glass window. Using what looked like a boat paddle, he flipped a behemoth slab of chocolate fudge cooling on the big marble table. Flipping fudge in windows was a great crowd pleaser on the island and sold a lot of fudge.

Restaurants and bars hummed with tourists bustling in and out. There were no motors, horns, or traffic lights with bikes, horses, and carriages as the approved modes of transportation on Fudge Island. The place was called that because the Good Stuff and seventeen other fudge shops sold tons of fudge to fudgies every year. The place should really be called Dentists' Paradise or Where Weight Watchers Comes to Die.

"Tell me you're not going to ride that thing," Nate Sutter said as he pedaled up beside me on his official, black bike with *Police* stenciled on the fender. "You'll weave, scream, wreck, and scare the heck out of the horses."

Nate Sutter was born and raised on the island. His mother owned the Good Stuff Fudge Shop next to the bike shop and was married to Rudy, my business partner. Sutter was now our vigilant and, most of the time, beloved police chief after a ten year detour with the Detroit PD. Due to my stubborn streak and black cloud condition and Sutter's equally stubborn streak plus being the sheriff, our paths crossed a lot. We had one of those *I can do anything you can do better* relationships. Although he was better at finding the bad guys, my way was more exciting and included Nutty Buddies.

Every female on the island regarded Sutter as one of those ruggedly handsome types that got women all hot and bothered without trying. There was talk of the island minting their own money so his likeness could be on the bills - face on the front, butt on the back. This is the kind of girl talk that goes on at the Stang on those long, cold, winter nights.

"Think of it this way," Sutter carried on. "Your lack of biking ability gives your shop a bad rep and that's bad for business. If there's one thing you care about, it's business."

"Biking season is only seven months long at best around here and that doesn't give me much time to make ends meet. And if you think I'm bad for business?" I got set for some wheedling even though I had forgotten the blasted award thing. "What about a guy prone on the dock, staring up at the stars and not in a *gee isn't this romantic* kind of way? My biking doesn't hold a candle to that and what have you found out about him, huh?" I threw in that last part hoping it sounded like ordinary conversation or as much as a conversation could sound normal when talking about a corpse.

"Doc Prichard's with him now."

"And you'll tell me what Doc finds out?" We stopped in front of the Seabiscuit Café. The scent of burgers and fries wafting out onto the porch along with strands of *American Pie* reminded me I was starving!

"Sure, I will."

"No, you won't. You're not going to tell me squat. You're going to give me the mushroom treatment, keep me in the dark and feed me manure. So, I'll tell you what I already know and I'm not going to stop. John/Larry was a dockhand working on *Barefoot Girl.*"

Sutter's lips thinned. "Stay out of this one, Chicago."

"He liked the island," I added in my best *I am not staying out of anything* voice. "Even came here to the island to visit on days off. That's strange, don't you think? Most deckhands go home or find the nearest bar or newest fling and you're ticked off at me for some reason and it has to do with Larry or John or whatever his name is. Since Fiona and I found him we owe him and I got this black cloud so maybe I caused it to happen and I need to make things right."

"Newsflash - clouds don't kill people."

"How do you know for sure? Things that we can't explain happen all the time especially on this island. Izzy McDonald's son finally got a job last week, Jennie over at Millie's on Main got my order right for the first time in two years, and the Captain's given up smoking and he seemed to like John so he was probably an okay guy. How'd somebody like that wind up dead on an island dedicated to escaping the real world and all things fudge?"

"This is a police matter and you are not the police."

"How about you could deputize me." I added a toothy grin for effect.

"How about law enforcement would never recover."

"If I don't help find who did this guy in my cloud could get worse. More bad stuff will happen around here. And

I'll be in your hair even more. Think of *that,*" I added, getting more ticked off by the minute. "And for your information, I am getting better at bike riding, a lot better, and I'll prove it."

"You don't have to do that. I believe you. You don't have to prove anything."

Pride edged out common sense and I straddled the bike, put my foot on the pedal, and shoved off. Granted five AM would be a better time than five PM to prove my case, but I was fed up with Sutter stonewalling me and I had to do something other than stand there and argue and get nowhere.

I dodged the local wagon taxi that transported folks from ferry dock to hotel at the rip-roaring speed of five miles per hour. I maneuvered around the kid on a red bike, though he actually did more of the maneuvering. I steered by a family crossing the street and only slightly clipped the old lady with the walker, but why-oh-why was there a delivery dray coming right at me with the biggest horses ever?

I hit the brakes, stifled a scream, and swerved onto Hoban Street with my back tire fishtailing. I sideswiped the pink rosebush in front of the Metivier Inn, missed the lethal pointy picket fence by a hair, and swung onto the side lane. The fact that it was secluded, free from gaping tourists, and had the medical center located at the end gave me some comfort. Nancy jumped the curb. Her tire hit a rock and together we crashed onto the grass next to a pot of red geraniums and white petunias. If I died here at least the flowers were already in place.

Panting, I flopped onto my back, staring up at the sky and ... at Bladen Powers shimmying down the ivy trellis on the side of the lovely Victorian hotel? A mid-thirties-ish woman with long blonde hair, wearing a white negligee and a really neat top hat of all things, waved at Bladen. She was partially hidden behind a potted palm on the second story balcony with an *Engaged Katie and Curtis* banner hanging from its railing. Bladen jumped from the trellis, flashed a grin at her, and waved back. Tucking in his shirt, he spotted me on the ground, winked at me, and jogged around to the back of the building. No wonder

Daniela didn't have a wedding cake, Powers was too busy playing patty cake with another bride-to-be.

A cyclist pulled up beside me and I crossed my fingers it was a sympathetic bystander offering a bottle of water. But deep down inside I knew it was Sutter. I braced myself for the *If that was doing better I'd hate to see worse*, but it never came. I cut my eyes to our dear police chief who was staring at the inn.

"What's he doing here?" Sutter said with a faraway look.

"I'm fine, thanks for asking. Your concern is so touching, memorable and heartfelt and just so you know, that guy running off is not Curtis from the Katie and Curtis banner. Bladen Powers is our resident wedding planner and troublemaker from Detroit and... You know him?"

That seemed to snap Sutter back into the present, and he looked down at me. "Why would I know a wedding planner from Detroit?"

"And why would you know a dead guy on the dock?"

"Do I?"

"Yes!"

"I gotta go." Sutter glanced back at the inn and grabbed his handlebars tighter. "Do us all a big favor and don't ride any more bikes."

"I own the shop!"

Muttering something about the *mysteries of the universe*, Sutter raced off while I stayed put waiting for my backbones to find their designated positions before I tried to stand. Sutter didn't deny he knew the dead guy or Powers. So, how did he know them? Did they all know each other? What would bring a cop, a wedding planner, and a dockworker together? It sounded like the beginning of a bad joke you told when half plastered. And why wouldn't Sutter tell me about it?

I pushed Nancy across the brick sidewalk toward the rear service entrance of the Metivier Inn. I parked the bike by the back door and rounded the far corner to take a shortcut to the Stang. Up ahead a party graced the side patio lit with candles and lanterns. Vases and bouquets of white flowers occupied every nook and cranny and a quartet played *When a Man Loves a Woman*. White-gloved waiters roamed about, plates and tableware clanked, glassed clinked, and a guy maybe in his early fifties sat alone at a head table with a *Katie and Curtis Forever* streamer across the front. Curtis's brows were knit, and he clutched an empty champagne glass in each hand. Did that bowtie hanging loose around his neck have little red bowler hats on it? And Katie had the top hat? A themed engagement party?

Looking for the shortcut, I cut across a rose garden then between a stack of firewood and row of boxwoods as, "Bladen, you are such a naughty, naughty boy ducking out in the middle of your event to be with me," came from the other side.

The middle bush rustled followed by more giggling and rustling and Bladen Powers whispering, "Only for you, babe. Only for you."

People were entitled to their privacy. I got that. The antics on the other side of the hedge were none of my business. I got that too. Except this was Mackinac where privacy didn't count for much and I personally knew how badly being two-timed sucked whether it was by World Series tickets or the resident wedding planner. Shoving aside the branches I came eye to eye with a woman. She yelped, I did the same, we both jumped, and Bladen Powers flipped off a hammock, landing face down on the ground.

"What in the world do you want?" the woman gasped as she stumbled to her feet. She straightened her black dress with frilly white maid apron and readjusted her starched white cap.

Bladen propped his head up on his hand. "You sure get around, bike lady. Got a lot of energy, do you?"

"Hey, I'm not the only one with surplus energy." I turned to the maid. "I'm here to drop off a bike for one of your guests."

"Do I look like I'm waiting for a blasted bike? I'm on my break! I'm allowed to have a break, any kind of break I want and some are a lot more fun than others." She winked at Bladen. "So you can get lost."

The maid tucked strands of hair under her cap while slipping on her left shoe. Bladen gave me a little finger wave then pointed toward the lane, suggesting I should leave. “Sticking your nose where it doesn’t belong can be bad for your health,” he sneered.

“So can sliding down the trellis. I bet that guy sitting over there at his engagement party on the patio - Curtis isn’t it, the guy with the cute bowtie? - might be wondering what’s keeping his lovely young fiancée. Katie, is it? Wearing a top hat? And a white negligee? Second floor balcony with the potted palm? Oh, and there she is now and looking a little disheveled.”

I pointed to the gal strolling across the patio. “I wonder what she did with the hat? And I wonder what she’s been up to? Got any ideas why she’s looking all flushed? Hey, Bladen, is that ivy stuck in your hair?”

Bladen reached for his hair that didn’t actually have ivy in it as the maid’s sexy grin vanished and she glared at Bladen. “*You’re* the one doing the fast and furious with our resident gold digger? You’re the one tearing up our trellis and smashing our flowers? You're giving our hotel a bad name. I could lose my job."

"But... But..." Bladen batted his lashes. "She seduced me. It's all her fault."

"Bunk! This is all bunk, isn't it." The maid's lip curled, her penciled-in brows narrowing. "You're not really going to hire me on, are you? I'm not going to be your new assistant? You're just playing me to get a little something on the side when you're already getting a whole lot of something on the side."

She stomped her foot. "I gave up Ralphie for you. Ralphie treated me good and we would have been married by now. Ralphie loved me and I fell for your bag of bologna and job with a promising career. You double-crossing, no-good... "

"Ignoramus," I chimed in.

"Yeah, that's what you are, a big old ignoramus." The maid yanked off her cap, threw it at Bladen, and kicked him in the butt. "No one plays Eileen Fisher. I bet the cook has a nice carving knife I could borrow or my daddy has a gun from when he was a soldier up at the fort."

"Now, just a minute." Bladen bolted straight up. I added, "I think we should just neuter him."

Eileen flashed me a big grin. "Now there's an idea." She turned for the gardening shack and called to me, "Hold him down, honey, and don't let him get away. I'll find the hedge clippers. That should do the trick."

"What?" Bladen jumped up, eyes bulging. "Wait. No. You can't do that. This was just a bit of fun."

"Fun? I'll show you fun." Eileen yanked open the door to the shed. "You better start sleeping with one eye open, Mr. Wedding Planner 'cause I got a little snip job planned and if I don't get you tonight there are other nights. I just love working nights." She wagged her brows and made a cutting motion with her fingers.

Bladen gave me an evil look and a hand gesture to match and hobbled off with his hand protecting the family jewels. Eileen gave me a little salute, closed the shed door, and skipped off to the patio. The island might have crappy cell phone service but the fudge vine was on high alert twenty-four-seven. By the time I got to the Stang the word would be out about sleazebag Bladen and his bed-hopping days would be history. Who knows, with all this free time, maybe the creep would have time to get Daniela a wedding cake after all.

I cut behind the historic Biddle House that still had a huge working fireplace where reenactors demonstrated cooking in the 1800s. They made the chicken soup in cast iron pots and their biscuits and apple butter were to die for. I came out on Market Street with lamplight dotting the sidewalk and the full moon low in a star-filled sky. The barn doors of the blacksmith shop were shut for the night, but faint whiffs of smoke from the dying forge still curled into the dark. Blacksmithing was another popular fudgie attraction with sparks flying, earsplitting hammering guaranteed to bring on a migraine, and glowing, red-hot metal.

A white clapboard building sat just ahead with the police station on the bottom floor, the courthouse on the second, and a hexagonal cupola perched on the roof. It was a charming one-stop-shop for bad guys with nab 'em, nail 'em, and jail 'em all in one place. No doubt Molly was on duty and Sutter wasn't, and I had a little time before meeting Fiona at the Stang. This was a great time to pump Molly for the latest info on the dead guy. Strawberry smoothies put Molly in a chatty mood, but with me having only a half-gone roll of cherry Lifesavers in my pocket I'd have to wing it.

I opened the door to the wood staircase on the left that led up to the courtroom. Pictures of grumpy Sutter, smiling Molly, and two part-time officers hung on the wall with the police reception desk straight ahead. Molly sat on one side of the desk cluttered with files, computer, phone, and a framed picture of Luca. She leaned across the desk, nearly touching noses with the actual, dreamy-eyed Luca sitting on the other side.

"Hi, guys." I flashed my best innocent, just-happened-to be-walking-by smile and added a little wave. "I stopped by to leave a note for Sutter that I have his award at the bike shop so he can pick it up and—"

"WowamIgladtoseeyou!" Molly jumped up from behind the desk, grabbing the phone and nearly pulling the whole thing onto the floor. She thrust the receiver in my hand. "We wanna go look at the moon."

"Is that code for necking?"

"Could be." Luca blushed and Molly added, "This stupid phone has a cord. Do you believe we live in a place that has cords on their phones? Duh! What year is this?"

"On Mackinac, nobody really knows."

Luca was tall, dark, and handsome, the nicest guy ever, and the youngest member of the Detroit 'family', if you know what I mean, who now graced Mackinac's sunny shores. He was an accountant. I guess he kept track of the family books and other stuff I didn't need to know about. That he dated a police officer seemed a bit problematic, but he and Molly and the IRS were making a go of it so who was I to judge.

Molly held the receiver with the cradle dangling

below, the whole thing looking like somebody had shot it and strung it up to display. "It won't reach all the way outside and now you're here to man the desk or, in this case, woman the desk. We need ten minutes alone, okay? Just ten."

"Maybe fifteen." Luca blushed again.

"You're the best." Giggling like a schoolgirl, Molly shoved the receiver in my hand and the two lovebirds raced outside with the door slamming closed behind them.

"No, *you're* the best especially right now," I said to the closed door. Pumping Molly for info wasn't going to work, but there were other ways to get the skinny on what was happening around here.

I reassembled the phone and unhooked the purple paperclips from my fleece. I counted to ten to give the lovebirds time to get moonstruck while I straightened the clips. Then I headed down the hall, my footsteps echoing through the quiet. Jail cells that were more Pottery Barn than black hole of Calcutta sat in the back with a meeting room to the right. On the left side was a wooden door with a top half of frosted glass and *Chief of Police Nate Sutter* scripted in black. Looked like Helvetica font. Personally, I would have gone with the classier Courier New.

I hunkered down in front of the door, jabbed the two wires into the lock, poked around hunting for the barrel and pins, and then gave a jab and a flip. The lock clicked. Feeling a little like Sherlock Holmes and a whole lot lucky, I stood, turned the handle, and walked in, leaving the office door open in case the phone rang.

Here's the thing. For sure Molly was a good source of island scuttlebutt, but Sutter's office was the Holy Grail. I turned on the banker's lamp with a brass base and a green glass shade. The desk was completely organized with pencils in holders, papers stacked in trays, computer shut down, and chair facing forward. Even the coffeepot sat on a pewter tray with six white mugs, their handles pointing in the same direction. Next to the pot was a stack of napkins spiraled out in a fan display. I'd seen this side of Sutter before. Nobody arranged flowers better than our police chief and there was no drippy paint can with notes taped to it in sight. How'd the man get anything done?

Anyone who fanned napkins and arranged pencils by size would have their laptop password protected, so any info there was safe from my prying eyes. I rummaged through the *In* box finding local business stuff and a stack of flyers announcing the Cop-For-A-Day raffle to raise money for the fort wall. I opened the top drawer to... a total disaster?

Pens, Post-Its, a wood ruler, a letter opener, and other office supplies were strewn everywhere. It looked as if someone threw in a grenade and shut the drawer quick. When Sutter was a kid and his Mom told him to clean his room, did he kick everything under the bed? Not that I would ever do such a thing.

The middle drawer was more of a mess with envelopes, tape, scissors, and the like. The bottom drawer contained files turned every which way looking as if someone had danced the tarantella on them. I pulled out the one marked Larry Corrigan/John Bernard and opened it on the desk.

Okay, so our guy's name was Larry Corrigan aka Larry Leadfoot aka John Mason Bernard, six feet tall with brown eyes and brown hair. What was with the Leadfoot? Race car driver? And he had a Detroit address. Latest record of employment was with Marquette Shipping as a coxswain and stevedore. I knew stevedore was a deckhand and coxswain sounded a little dirty but that was probably my mind doing a fast slide into the gutter. I pulled out Sheldon and snapped a pic of this page before flipping to the next.

The cause of death was blunt force trauma - two blows to the head. Pinewood fragments were found in the wound. Maybe from a board pulled from a shipping pallet? Pallets were cheap pine. John had some minor drunk and disorderly offenses and an impressive number of speeding tickets. The king of pedal-to-the-metal leading to Leadfoot? The list of personal effects included the champagne, money clip, watch, knife, and wallet with its contents. A generic photo of John, probably from his employer, was stapled to the folder, and a phone number was clipped to the top sheet. I took pictures of everything, clicked off the desk light, and then stopped dead, staring into the dark. I turned around, clicked on the light, and opened the top desk drawer again.

Chapter Four

I picked up the wood letter opener, except it wasn't a wood-handled letter opener. It was a closed knife lying on top of a letter opener. The knife was exactly like the one we found on John and it had the same date inscribed... Maybe? I snapped a picture of the knife. See, here's where Sherlock Holmes and I parted company. Sherlock would have noticed the date on John's knife when we were on the dock and remembered it. I had forgotten what I had for lunch or even if I had lunch.

The information in the folder included the knife but not the inscribed date, so I couldn't compare the two. John's stuff was locked up in the evidence room. If the two dates matched, the odds were good that Sutter and John had been in the same wedding. This meant that they for sure knew each other, just as I suspected.

Yeah, yeah, yeah. There was more than one wedding on any given day. I got that. But what were the chances of more than one wedding on the same day giving the same gift to those in the wedding party? I turned to the closet behind me where Sutter locked up evidence and probably his chocolate chip cookie stash since many in town had been known to swipe their fair share...or so I heard.

I had to get inside the closet, locate the evidence, check the date on John's knife, and it was my duty to take a cookie or two to help preserve Sutter's muscles and his nice butt. Brandishing my two paperclips, I walked over to the evidence closet and stopped dead. Sutter had a Yale lock on that door, and it was no run of the mill Yale lock! This one was thick, serious, of the heavy-duty variety, and out of my league, which was Lock Picking 101.

Molly and Luca were due back and it would probably take me about three weeks to figure out how to pick the Yale. I had to get out of here now. If Molly found me snooping she'd tell Sutter and he'd have me in his crosshairs wondering what I was up to next. I hooked my paperclips back on my fleece, turned off the desk lamp, and headed for the reception desk just as the lovers moseyed it hand-and-hand.

“Thanks, Evie,” Molly hummed without looking at me. “I owe you.”

“Ya know, I’ve been thinking,” I said in my best casual voice, not that Molly or Luca would notice the world coming to an end in their present enamored state. “There was a knife on that guy John we found on the dock last night. It had a date inscribed on it.”

“Sure thing.” Molly smiled up at Luca.

“The date inscribed looked familiar and I think we might have been at that same wedding. And maybe,” I pushed on, “I ran into the dead guy somewhere. Or maybe we knew some of the same people and they might have an idea why someone would be out to knock him off. Could you get that date for me?”

“Sure thing.” Molly wrapped her arms around Luca’s waist.

“The knife is probably locked up in the evidence closet.”

“Sure thing.” Luca wrapped his arms around Molly.

“And don’t say anything to Sutter,” I tossed in. “I don’t want him to think I’m on to something if I’m not and ... the jail is on fire and Captain America is coming to put it out and maybe we should call Spiderman just in case.”

“Sure thing,” Luca and Molly said together. Molly giggled and kissed Luca and any chance of Molly or Luca remembering anything I said or me getting any information vanished into thin air.

I headed for the door, closed it behind me, and started for the Stang. Maybe Fiona had had better luck and found something out about John on her delivery rounds like how could he possibly know Sutter? Sutter was a cop and John was a deckhand and even if he had another job in Detroit, what could possibly bring these two together? There was no mention of a criminal record in John’s file so it’s not like Sutter had arrested him. But Sutter knew John as Larry and no way was it mistaken identity and...

“Praise the Lord and light the candles! Wait ‘til you see what I found!” Fiona gushed as she yanked me onto the Stang porch, nearly crashing into three patrons coming out. “You won’t believe it, Evie. This is really terrific, I mean like the best thing ever to happen to me in a long time, maybe ever.”

“You got proof Sutter knew John?”

“John who?” Fiona waved her hands in the air as if shooing a fly. “I had to come out here to cool off. I’m having a hot flash, the good kind.” She fluffed her blouse to catch the evening breeze then grabbed the front of my jacket and pulled me close. “I think I’m in love.”

“I didn’t even know you were seeing someone.”

“Well, I have been for about twenty minutes now. You can tell a lot in twenty minutes.” Fiona opened the red door, took my hand, and hauled me past the juke box blaring *Brown-Eyed Girl*, past the big yellow airplane propeller hanging on the wall, and turned me around to face the jam-packed noisy bar area. “Look at him. Isn’t he yummy! I think I’m going to faint.”

“Which yummy are we talking about?”

“Sexy as hell, right there,” she said over the din. She nodded at a table underneath the picture of the P-51

Mustang fighter plane that the original owner flew in the Korean War.

"He's old."

"Forty is not old."

I gave her a hard look.

"Okay, maybe forty-five-ish and he's lean and fit and drop-dead gorgeous and has the best smile ever. Just look at that wavy hair all mussed up like he doesn't care and he has blue eyes. I adore blue eyes. We've been talking and he's the one, *my* one. And he keeps giving me the look." Fiona put her hand to her heart to catch her breath. "I want you to meet him but I've got dibs so don't try anything cute to win him over, okay?"

"Full moons should be outlawed. So," I rushed on, "did you find out anything about dead dock guy and Sutter?"

Fiona ogled the new guy in town, a little drop of drool at the corner of her mouth. "Who cares about a dead guy, I got myself a live one! Let me introduce you. I told him we were friends and that I went to school with Nate. He's Mr. Friendly, he wants to meet everyone."

"I need to make a phone call."

"Gives me more time alone with my man. He's here to visit Nate and he's going to some fancy wedding at the fort with period dress, soldier reenactments, and cannon blasts and I'm going with him and did I mention I'm in love?"

"You hate reenactments."

"I need a dress. Something old, something blue. Sounds like a wedding dress. My wedding dress."

"Since when have you been interested in getting married?"

"Since about twenty minutes ago." Fiona fluffed her short bob again and sashayed her way over to the table. I headed for the bar and asked Scooter for a Miller Lite. What I really wanted was a vodka something to help deal with everyone else being all hormone happy and not having two gray cells to rub together and me getting nowhere fast on the dead guy/Sutter case. I asked Scooter if I could use the landline sitting at the end of the bar and he gave me a thumbs-up.

Scooter was a thirtyish *come-here* like me except he was trying to escape a scheming mom who wanted him to be a surgeon and marry an heiress. Amazing what you find out about people over brews and a plate of fried green beans. My mother, on the other hand, bribed my fiancé to *not* marry me, had a law office behind the bike shop, and thanked the heavens every day I was not a lawyer since my cloud and I considered everyone guilty until proven innocent and I couldn't lie for beans.

I hitched up onto a barstool, pulled out Sheldon, and flipped through my pictures until I got to the ones from Sutter's office. I dialed the number from the folder. Using a landline I had a fighting chance of connecting. I slid Sheldon in my jacket pocket and took a sip of beer while listening to the phone ring. I craned my neck around the burly tourist guy sitting next to me to get a better look at Fiona's latest heartthrob. Yep, he was fit - I had to give him that - and good-looking and he was taking his phone from his pocket. He answered it at the same time "Finn here" came over the phone in my hand.

What the heck! Did Fiona's guy just say *Finn here* into *his* phone the exact time I heard it on my phone? Finn looked at me, I looked at him, and holy freaking cow Finn was now heading right for me. He stopped in front of my stool and held up his phone with *Mustang Lounge* and the phone number right there on the screen.

"Caller ID?" I gulped.

"When calling from a landline the name of the business shows up. Don't you love modern technology?"

"Not at the moment."

There was a twinkle in Finn's blue eyes. "So, who are you, why are you calling me, and how'd you get my number?"

Okay, this guy had to be a suspect. I mean, why else would Sutter have his phone number attached to the folder? But Finn didn't have to know he was a suspect. If he found out, it could ruin Sutter's case and my chance to find out who the heck this guy really was and his connection to John. *Think, Evie, think*. Where did people get random phone numbers?

"Bathroom wall," I blurted. "Your number was on the bathroom wall under *Life of the Party*." I slid off the stool just as Sutter came into the Stang saying, "Hey, Finn. Sorry I'm late."

With Finn distracted for a split second, I hustled outside onto the porch and tried to ignore the footsteps following right behind me. I spun around to find … Scooter?

"Hey, just thought you should know that the guy you were talking to, the one with Fiona? He's a cop. Detroit. I saw his badge when he opened his wallet to pay for drinks. You looked kind of rattled and I thought you should know."

"He's here for a wedding."

Scooter gave a little shrug. "Maybe. The island isn't exactly where cops come for R and R even if he does know Nate. There's something going on with him besides brews and backslapping."

I stepped closer. “Did you know the dead guy found on the freight dock? Did he ever come in here?”

“Once or twice. He was looking for some dude. Had a picture of a groomed metro sexual with a blond-streaked ponytail and fake tan wearing a white dinner jacket.”

Scooter raked back his shaggy hair, his brow knit in thought. “He said the two of them worked the docks together but anyone that prissy would get the crap kicked out of ‘em on a loading dock so that’s bogus. You know, the face looked kind of familiar but I couldn’t place him. It’s been bugging me.”

“Did he mention champagne?”

Scooter laughed. “That goes with the prissy look for sure, but the Stang isn’t a champagne kind of place. I am experimenting with some small-batch brews to add to our drinking pleasure. Mackinac Moonlight, a pale ale, and Hops and Horses, more of a lager.”

“What about Cycles and Sinners?”

“You’re on. Going to print up my own labels with Scooter’s Brews right on the front.”

"No surgeon?"

"That's the only profession where you can stick knives in people legally."

Yuck! "Small batch is a great idea."

Scooter hustled back inside and I stepped off the porch and waited for a taxi to trot pass. Scooter was right. What was a Detroit cop doing here at this particular time? The wedding? Maybe, but he didn't have a date with him. My guess was that Finn had something to do with Sutter and Dead John and the wedding was a cover. Why did Finn need a cover? Why did Sutter?

I turned onto Main as a group of fudgies bolted out of Horn's Bar laughing and running full-out for the docks trying to make the ferry. That's the thing about an island. You miss the last boat and you're stuck here 'til morning unless you're really good at the backstroke.

Up ahead, strollers ambled though Marquette Park and a not-so-great jazz quartet warbled in the gazebo. I turned into Doud's Market, the island's answer to the mall, and got a slice of pizza for me and two cans of Fancy

Feast to prevent an evening gripe fest of meowing by poor, mistreated felines. I may own the bike shop plus residence, but truth be told I knew who ruled the Bloomfield roost and it sure as heck wasn't me.

It was well past six, the time my cardboard clock on the door said I would return. Two bikes were parked on the porch with notes from customers saying they'd be back tomorrow to get their deposits. I unlocked the door and flipped on the lights to find Bambino and Cleveland sitting on the pool table with beady eyes, twitching tails, and accusing sneers. Fiona and others got sweet purring kitties and snuggles; I got judgment at Nuremburg and *feed me mow*.

"I know I'm late," I said while scooping gross-smelling smooshy stuff into bowls by the workbench. "And you're right, I did crash the bike, but the bike is okay and look," I held up my arms. "No scrapes – well, no new ones - and I am getting better. I missed the concrete and landed on the grass and I brought you dinner so enough with the stink eye."

The fury twosome jumped from their perch, the lure of whatever the heck they put in Fancy Feast winning out over criticizing me at least for the next five minutes. I wolfed down the pizza, rolled in the returned bikes, and parked them in the line of rentals. I then headed to the back of the shop for two rusted bikes restored by Cal, my Mr. Bike Wizard. Cal got the dents out of vintage, abused bikes and I painted ‘em up all adorable. Not exactly a Warren Buffett operation, but with my graphic design freelancing jobs in the winter, I managed to keep Rudy’s Rides up and running, or at least limping along.

To get moving on the bride and groom bikes, I lugged the two rusted Schwinn Starfire frames into a little makeshift paint booth I’d jerry rigged with boards so as not to spray paint the whole shop along with myself. I pried open a can of dull red primer, stirred, and dumped it into the sprayer. I plugged it in and hit the trigger, testing the narrow spray pattern on an old newspaper as the bell over the front door tinkled.

“Be with you in a minute. I need to get the first coat of paint on these bikes so it’ll dry and—”

"Bathroom wall? That's the best you could do?"

I spun around and sprayed a neat red stripe of primer across the front of Finn's navy windbreaker, his neck, and a bit of his lower chin. "Holy crap! Why are you here?"

Chapter Five

Finn swiped at his chin, the paint now covering his fingertips. "At least I won't rust? Nate said you were a pain in the backside and if there was trouble you'd be in the thick of it." Finn rocked back on his heels. "So, you and Nate are an item?"

"If you mean we get in each other's way, then yeah. And as for me being a pain?" For a second there I'd felt really bad about the paint, but now not so much. "You're the one who snuck up on me. And why are you here on the island now when we have a guy toes-up on the dock. Coincidence? I don't think so and if you dare hurt Fiona," I took a step closer since I was on a tirade, "I'll feed you to the fishes myself."

"Smart girl." Finn laughed and grabbed a handful of paper towels off the workbench. He swiped at his jacket, only managing to smear the primer over a larger area. "But before you throw me in the lake, consider the fact that I'm here because you and I are on the same side. I like Fiona and you like Fiona. I like Nate and you like Nate and how'd you really get my number and why did you call it?"

Aha! I was right. Finn didn't deny his showing up had something to do with Dead John, but now for the tricky part of giving up a little info to find out more. "I got your number from Dead John's file that just happened to be open at the police station when I just happened to be visiting."

"You are a really bad liar. And why would a bike shop owner care about a dead guy on the docks? Island boredom?"

"Island black cloud." I set the spray gun on the workbench before I caused any more damage. "I've been here over two years and have three dead bodies to show for it. Before my arrival, the last murder was back in the sixties when Mabel Farnswarth caught her husband with the librarian who was stacked better than the Library of Congress, or so the story goes."

Cleveland and Bambino circled my ankles. “If I help find who did in John maybe my bad karma will lighten up and so will the body count. I haven’t swung a dead cat under a full moon to break the spell yet, mostly because I like cats, but so far nothing’s helped.”

“And?”

“And I think Sutter’s connected to John but he won’t tell me how. His mother and I are friends. She lost her husband a few years back and she doesn’t need anything to happen to her son.”

A little smile played at the corner of Finn’s mouth. “Never mess with a woman on a mission. Two ex-wives and one ex-dog taught me that.”

Finn rubbed the back of his neck. “Okay, here goes. Only because you stumbling around and kicking up dirt won’t help anybody. Hope this doesn’t bite me in the butt. Nate worked undercover in Detroit. Things went south and five million went missing. John was part of the gang and was no doubt looking for the money. For some reason it led him here. I was Nate’s contact when he was undercover and feel responsible. Whoever really ran off with the money is looking for Nate too. Nate ruined a sweet operation in Detroit and he knows all the players. Thought I'd pay a friendly visit and keep an eye out."

"Sutter did undercover as in drugs? Guns? The mob?"

"Let's just say we called him the planner."

"Shutthefrontdoor, it *is* the mob."

"Not exactly. Look, the locals won't talk to me and Sergeant Molly's taken up permanent residence on the Love Boat, but I bet everyone around here is used to the annoying gal painting me red and poking around in everybody's business and being a pest."

"Let's go with adorably inquisitive."

That brought another smile. "If you can find out who John was looking for, that could lead us to who took the money and the killer and get Nate off the hook. Nate thinks he can do this himself, but I'm not so sure. He can't be everywhere at once and this place is tourist central."

"For openers we need to keep this just between us. If Sutter finds out what we're up to he'll have an aneurysm and you'll be on the first ferry out of here."

"And I need to be here. This could be dangerous and I need to watch your back." Finn shoved his hands in his jean pockets and studied the floor.

"Good grief. There's more?"

"Uh, maybe. Uh, what kind of flowers does Fiona like? Thought I'd...well...you know." Red inched up Finn's neck into his cheeks. For a second there he didn't look Detroit-cop at all but more like a man totally smitten.

"The kind that's from a man with a hint of Irish in his blood and a bit of mischief in his eyes."

Finn grinned, added a two-finger salute, and was out the door, the bell tinkling as he left. I could see Finn and Sutter as pals, and the fact that Finn was here on his own time to help said a lot about the guy. That he had a thing for Fiona and wanted to please her with special flowers was pretty much the icing on the cake. Some girls had all the luck and this time it was Fiona's turn. Yippee!

"Dang, girl. These bikes are fine," Cal said as he rolled in the front door and flipped the *Closed* sign to *Open* even though it wasn't yet eight o'clock. A lot of riders liked to get an early start on the day since no one had ever explained to them the joys of room service and sleeping in on vacation.

"Bet you were up all night painting these sweet wedding rides?" Cal added.

"They're for a hell-on-wheels bride having her wedding up at the fort and I bet you were up all night too. I saw the new cashier at Doud's giving you the eye when she was in here yesterday," I countered as Cal maneuvered his way to the lower workbench.

"Not my type and I think I met the hell-on-wheels gal." Cal spooned coffee into the maker with Bambino and Cleveland perched beside it, supervising. Cal clicked on the Mr. Coffee, and the hissing and gurgling sounds along with smells of morning filled the shop.

“Not only is she having her wedding up at the fort, but somehow she managed to get it closed early to tourists. She must have some juice to pull that one off and she’s demanding the soldiers form a musket arch and fire the cannon after the ceremony. We took up a collection for her life-size cutout so we got something to aim at.”

“Live ammo?”

“Some of the men use their muskets for hunting so it’s worth considering. The only reason we’re going along with this is that she’s donating family journals, china, a fife and drum set, and a pistol or two from when her relatives lived at the fort in the 1800s. She’s insisting on a brass donation plaque with her name, but all things considered, it’s a good addition to the fort museum.”

Cal’s day job was island employment, sort of a clearinghouse for matching seasonal workers with seasonal jobs. With fifteen-thousand tourists a day, there were a ton of jobs. Cal worked for me because a lot of cute girls rented bikes. He was a ripped, badass dude born and raised on the island except for the four tours of duty in Iraq that landed him on wheels. He considered this situation a minor inconvenience. We all considered Cal a major hero.

Cal put a mat on the workbench so as not to scratch my new paint job then propped up the bride bike and maneuvered a new tire into place. “So did you happen to meet that cop guy from Detroit?” There was a slight hitch in Cal’s voice. “What’s his story?”

“Seems that Sutter was undercover as a mob boss, things fell apart, and the bad guys might be hunting him. Finn’s here to lend a hand.”

“Sounds like an okay guy.”

“And he’s got a thing for Fiona.”

Cal growled, “I heard that.” There was another hitch in his voice. “Gee, what’s taking that coffeemaker so darn long this morning. It’s slow as molasses.”

I put down the white whicker basket that we would fasten to the handlebars and stared at Cal. “Slow as molasses? Darn? Gee? Have you ever said gee in your life? And you’re not looking at me or smiling and if you grip that wrench any tighter you’ll bend it. Are you worried about

Sutter? Yeah, I am too but this Finn guy knows what he's doing and... Oh, boy," I added in a long drawn out voice. "This has nothing to do with Sutter. You like her. This is all about Fiona. You like Fiona."

Cal reached for a set of sockets. "Everybody likes Fiona."

"Yeah, but you really *like* her. Does she know?" I thought about that for a split second. "Of course she doesn't know," I reasoned. "She would have said something to me between *There's a dead guy on the dock* and *Why don't you pay for delivery like everybody else*. She would have tossed in *I think Cal's into me, isn't that great*."

"Yeah and what if she didn't think it's so great and none of this is your business."

"What planet do you live on?" I grabbed two mugs and poured. "This is Mackinac, where gossip's on twenty-four/seven. Since rumor has it that the only thing you can't do is climb stairs," I gave him a sexy wink and handed him a mug, "you have to tell her how you feel, my friend."

"Tell who what," Fiona gushed as she waltzed into the shop. Cal gave me a hard look that said *keep your mouth shut* while shaking his head.

"Tell you that I'm in love?" Fiona carried on. She did a pirouette that was probably a throwback to some grade school dance lessons. "Because I am in love, totally and completely." She danced over to Cal, sat on his lap and slipped her cap backwards on his head. "Aren't you happy for me, my man?"

"Thrilled." Cal reached around her to tighten a bolt on the bike and Fiona kissed him on the forehead, leaving behind a pink lipstick kiss.

"And I'm thrilled too. I'm thrilled to my toes and beyond." She jumped up and gulped down my coffee. "And to show you just how happy I am, I'm here this bright beautiful morning to invite you both to a little get-together at the Stang tonight, all my treat."

I stared at Fiona wide-eyed. "Two nights ago I had to bribe you with dinner at the Village Inn so you'd take me to get the kites."

"And look how that turned out. I should have gotten a month of free beers at the Stang to go with it for the PTSD I'm suffering, but I forgive you because I'm such a sweetheart. Well, Finn thinks I am and that's all that counts."

"And now you're springing for a party," I said, still in shock. "As in picking up the tab and actually paying it and not pretending to lose your purse like you usually do? So who the heck are you and what have you done with Fiona?"

"Think of it as my good deed for the day for you and all of my friends and if you must know I'm out to impress the new bf...that's code for boyfriend, something I haven't had in a while, a really long while."

"Now how do you know there's not some secret admirer out there just pining for you?" That got me an evil look from the military section of the shop.

"Because on this island there are no secrets and meeting Finn is my destiny." Fiona stood and pranced over to the coffeepot. She poured a refill into my mug and took a sip. “He’s here to help find some bad people who are after Nate, but don’t tell anyone that. The less people who know the better so no one gets hurt trying to play hero.” She clutched the mug to her chest and heaved a sign. “And speaking of heroes, isn’t Finn just terrific? What a babe! What a hunk!”

“Mr. Wonderful, I’m sure,” Cal murmured, tackling the bike tire like an angry sumo wrestler.

“And my plan is for him to see me as fun-loving, carefree, spontaneous, and whimsical as well as an egg-head newspaper editor. That’s why I’m doing the party thing and why I’ve got an appointment at Village Glam for one of their super-duper mani-pedi packages. I want to look all sexy tonight and I’m busting out a new perfume I got for Christmas. Cleopatra.”

“I gave you that perfume,” Cal muttered.

“Now all I need is a boat down the Nile, or in this case Lake Huron, and I think I’ll skip the snake part and...” Fiona’s voice trailed off, giving way to loud arguing coming from outside the shop.

"What's going on now?" Fiona tsked. "Can we all say anger management class?" Fiona headed for the door. "But until that happens, God forbid we miss anything. Come on you two." Fiona arched her arm in follow me fashion. "Usually we have to wait until noon around here for some decent drama to jumpstart the day."

Cal followed Fiona and I tagged along out onto the porch. Byline stood behind a dray loaded with crates of chardonnay from Sandhill Crane Vineyards while Bladen Powers paced alongside. His forehead was wrinkled, his eyes deep set, and today he didn't look a thing like Don Juan scampering down the trellis and waving farewell to a fair maiden in her top hat.

"I've got enough to deal with right now," Bladen groused to the woman standing beside him as morning strollers meandered down the street and a long blast from a ferry horn sounded from the passenger dock in the heart of town. "You'll have to pick up the slack, Petula, until I can figure out where we go from here and..."

Bladen stopped midsentence when he saw me. He took a step back and held his clipboard below his waist like a shield. “Look,” he said to me, his voice shaky. “I’m here on business, I swear, nothing more, and I really don’t need any more problems right now.”

He took another step back, swallowed, and said to Petula. “This is the woman I was telling you about who can maybe help. She got the bride and groom bike situation straightened out with Daniela, so maybe she can save your butt this time too. Just don’t give her any grief. She looks harmless enough, but she’s got a mean real streak. I speak from experience.”

“Honey, my butt is just fine and dandy, thank you very much,” Petula hissed. She kissed her palm and smacked her backside. “We’re talking about your butt being on the line due to that there other equipment in your southern regions that never takes a rest. I bet dollars to doughnuts that’s what got us into this fine predicament. And don’t you dare go dumping this cake fiasco on me like you did at that Feinstein affair. Wedding Wonderland almost fired me over that little incident.”

“Hey, I saved your job, didn’t I?” Bladen huffed.

"Only 'cause you need me." Petula swiped back a clump of straggly brown hair that hadn't seen a shampoo bottle or comb in a while. "And it's more like I saved yours job. Fact is, I should have your job and maybe one of these days I will. I do most of the work anyway. If I hadn't called Reverend Ellis last night to remind the man that the wedding was at the fort tomorrow, there'd be no wedding, just a fuming bride ready to disembowel you on the spot. And whatever did you go and do at the Metivier Inn? Now Curtis is flat out refusing to pay us a single penny. He's threatening to sue."

Bladen opened his mouth and Petula held up her hand as if stopping a freight train. "Right now we need to concentrate on the cake getting to the fort tomorrow and the tables and those cute little white chairs set up on the parade ground for dinner."

"And we need bunting across the porch railings and a floral archway for the ceremony," Bladen tossed in. "I know this is a high profile wedding and if it blows up, no one will ever hire us again and--."

"And if it does blow up, I intend to strangle you with my bare hands. We need that cake pronto! So," Petula said turning to Cal, Fiona and me, "bless your little old Michigan hearts for being here. Do any of you fine folk know how to bake?"

Chapter Six

"I can slice a mean Pillsbury cookie dough roll," Fiona offered. I added, "Sara Lee is the best," while Cal chimed in with, "I do a great Pop-Tart."

"But," Cal held up his hand when it looked as if Petula might faint dead on the spot. "Don't go jumping off Arch Rock just yet, there are people with those with skills on the island. We got Irish Donna over at the Blarney Scone right 'round the corner. I bet for the right price and a lot of flattery she can fix you up with a wedding cake."

Petula brightened. "Well, I'll be a monkey's uncle."

Cal hitched his chin toward Main Street. "Come on, I'll show you the way. Besides, you'll need someone to protect you from husband Shamus, king of the wandering eye and fast hands."

Petula twitched her hips. "Honey, I'm not so sure I want all that protecting. Sounds like a fun way to start the day if you ask me."

"Take the protection," Fiona offered as Bladen reached into his pocket, pulled out a silver dollar money clip, and peeled off five one-hundred dollar bills.

Fiona's jaw dropped as she stared at the money clip. Her gaze fused with mine as Bladen handed the money to Petula. "Here's enough for a down payment on the cake. They can invoice me later for the rest."

"You better darn well make sure you have the sage green and cream linens for the tables tomorrow," Petula called over her shoulder as she and Cal crossed Main Street. "Any of this goes wrong and Daniela will have you facing the firing squad and those good ol' boys up at the fort have the guns to do the job right."

Bladen snarled, took two more steps away from me, climbed onto the dray, and glanced around. "Okay, so where the heck did the driver go? He was just here and I'm paying him by the hour and we need to get this wine to the dock right now."

"Hey, Bladen," Fiona started, "by any chance did you happen to know that guy Joh—"

"Otis," I blurted and kicked Fiona in the shins. "He makes great coffee over at Doud's across the street and you really should get to know him. I bet that's where your driver is. Everyone loves Otis's coffee."

"And the driver's probably shooting the breeze," Bladen huffed and climbed off the dray. "That's all you people do around here. Now I got to find him and get this champagne out of the sun before that goes right to hell too."

Bladen stomped off toward Doud's and Fiona rubbed her shins growling, "Why'd you kick me? I saw the money clip and so did you and it was the same as John's. I was going to ask Bladen if he knew John and you know he does. The clip is dead on proof and--"

"And what if Bladen's the killer, huh? Did you think of that?" I said in a hushed whisper. "If we ask him a bunch of questions then he'll know we're on to him and that could be real bad for our health."

Fiona parked her hand on her hip. "You seriously think pretty boy Bladen is the killer? Girl, from what I hear that man's a lover not a fighter, and besides that, why would he kill John?"

"I don't know about the why, but the how is easy enough. It doesn't take much to bonk someone on the head. It's not like stabbing where blood spurts everywhere."

"Thank you so much for that delightful image at eight in the morning."

"Are you sure you're a reporter? John worked the docks," I went on, trying to figure things out. "Bladen got deliveries there and they both have the same money clip. I bet Captain knows if there's a connection between those two. Not much gets past the man."

I shimmied into her carriage and Fiona didn't budge. "Well, what are you waiting for?" I grumped. "Come on, make Byline go. We need to get to the dock. Cal will be back in a few minutes to run the shop, so I can leave now. This is our best lead yet. Get a move on."

"I really do have a newspaper to run, you know."

"And you have your mani-pedi appointment to squeeze in and you need time to primp, and you don't want to go anywhere right now, I get it. But think of this, do you really want to impress the new BF? What if we find the killer, that'll impress the bejeebers out of him? Brains and beauty, right? Aren't brains the new sexy these days?"

"Actually, I think a push-up bra and bikini panties from Victoria Secret are, but okay, okay, I'll go and just for the record, what the heck's a bejeeber? I don't think I have one so how can it get scared out of me?"

"This is what I get for being friends with an English major. Just put the pedal to the metal or whatever. Why in the world aren't there cup holders in a buggy? I could really do with a cup of Otis's coffee."

Fiona hoisted herself into the carriage. "Any more caffeine and I'd make you get out and push. Did you notice that Bladen didn't look nearly as handsome today?" Fiona flicked the reins and Byline trotted off. “I think his hair is thinning and he’s getting a fat-man paunch.”

“You think that because you now have Finn the fabulous in your life.”

Fiona grinned and batted her eyes. “Ain’t life grand?”

We clip-clopped passed the gazebo then Marquette Park as Main turned into Lake Shore. The public docks with pleasure boats bobbing in the gentle waves sat to the right and a taxi headed for the ferries coming into port and loaded with fudgies passed us on the left. “So, just how much do you like this Mr. Fabulous?”

“We… get along.” Fiona steered around two bikers with balancing problems even worse than mine then we took the bend for Mission Point as a V of geese cut across the bright blue sky. “He makes an effort, he always smells good, he lets me know he cares, he’s a friend to Nate so you know he’s one of the good guys, and he makes me laugh. He brought me flowers. Sunflowers.” Fiona had a dreamy look in her eyes. “He said I’m his Michigan sunshine.”

"A Detroit cop said *that*?"

"Exact words." We turned down the lane toward the freight dock.

"Are we really *sure* this guy's a Detroit cop?"

"Got the scars to prove it." Fiona laughed and blushed. "I can attest to that firsthand."

The scent of diesel hung in the air as a gray cloud of exhaust billowed off the port bow of a cargo ferry motoring away from the pier. Or maybe it was that the stern side of the boat that had the exhaust? Why they just didn't say front and back like everyone else and-- "It's *Barefoot Gal*."

"As in the fourth race at Hialeah?"

"As in the boat John worked on." I jabbed my finger toward the dock. "And she's getting away."

I slapped my palm to my forehead. "I didn't think about the boat coming back here! How could I not think of that? It's not like boats leave port and drop off the end of the earth never to return. Nancy Drew would have thought of the boat returning and so would have Sherlock Holmes," I whined. "We could have asked around, see what her captain and dockhands had to say. We could have gotten some great info."

"Oh, yeah, because dockhands have so much to say to a reporter and her friend when they're hustling around unloading freight."

"Hey, we could have strutted our stuff. We're still young. We could have used our womanly wiles. Guys can get real chatty over wiles."

"*Are you looking for a good time, baby* is not the kind of chatty we need right now." Fiona pulled to a stop in front of the corrugated metal warehouse, with dockhands hoisting crates and boxes onto waiting drays to make daily deliveries to shops and hotels.

"I was wondering when you'd show up." Captain chomped his unlit cigar, readjusted his beat-up seaman's hat, and ambled down the lane toward us. Fiona tied up Byline and stepped out of the way of the workers. Big wagons lined the lane on either side as behemoth horses shook their heavy leather harnesses. A few drank from water troughs, which were everywhere on the island. Water troughs here were like gas stations in other towns, only they smelled better. Then again, some of the natural habits of horses didn't smell all that great either.

"Why'd you think we'd be coming?" I asked Captain while hopping down from the carriage.

"Nate. He said the two biggest busybodies on the island would be showing up this morning with *Barefoot Gal* being in port."

Ugh! Even Sutter thought I'd pick up on the returning boat thing.

"And I am supposed to tell you to..." Captain went on as he flipped back a paper on his clipboard and read, "To mind your own business for a change, stop pestering people, and let the police take care of things." Captain chuckled. "Nate's words, not mine."

"Okay, we can do that," I said and Fiona added, "We can?"

I flashed my goody-two-shoes smile. “We don’t want to upset anyone or get in the way of the police and we can mind our own business. But...”

Captain rocked back on his heels. “I can’t wait to hear this *but*.”

“But maybe we can do it a little later. Right now we’re wondering if there’s a connection between John the dead guy and Bladen Powers, that new wedding planner here on the island.”

“Maybe.” Captain stood on one foot then the other and shrugged his shoulders.

“And?”

Captain puffed on his cigar that wouldn’t puff and grinned.

“So, what’s it going to cost me to find out about the connection?”

“A Daniel Tiger kite. My little Effie loved the kite you gave me, but she’d really love one of Daniel Tiger.”

"Hello Kitty's big brother?" Fiona asked. "I never did get the white cat and a pink bow thing."

"Daniel's on TV. He tells kids to mind their manners, eat their vegetables, and return library books on time. Effie would get a big kick out of a Daniel Tiger kite."

"Sutter didn't have to bribe you with a kite," I groused.

"Sutter has a badge, a gun, and a jail cell." Captain took another non-drag off his cigar. "When that Bladen guy showed up this morning, he asked where John was, and I remembered those two knew each other. Maybe not well, like exchanging Christmas cards, but they talked. John helped Bladen load and unload the liquor when he didn't have to, guess that's how they got friendly. Anyway, this morning Bladen was real upset when he found out about John being dead and took right off without unloading that wine he had on his wagon. Can't say if this means anything one way or the other but—"

"But what does Bladen have to unload? He picks up stuff like wedding supplies."

"If he orders too much liquor, he sends cases back. That's what all the venues on the island do unless it's some popular booze they can hold onto for another affair. It costs money and it takes a bit of time to return orders to Detroit but it's better than letting inventory sit around and go bad. Remember, you promised the kite. Daniel Tiger. Don't forget."

Whistling, Captain headed for the warehouse, checking his clipboard. I turned to Fiona. "Holy cow, John and Bladen did for sure know each other and—"

"Not here," Fiona hissed. "We're attracting attention and looking a little conspicuous."

We got in the carriage and Fiona maneuvered around the big drays as if she'd done it all her life, which she had. I couldn't even parallel park a Honda Civic... when I had a Honda Civic.

"Okay, so John and Bladen had a connection," I said as Byline hoofed his way up the lane to the main road. "And the two had the same money clip. They could have been in the same wedding, but since when do a swanky wedding planner and dockworker called Leadfoot run in the same social circles?"

"They don't. Gifts, maybe?" Fiona steered past the white clapboard Old Mission Church with its octagonal wood belfry and past the cut off for the butterfly house. "Maybe Bladen gave the money clip, flask, and knife to John for helping him with loading and unloading? Bladen's a wedding planner and there could have been leftovers from a cancelled wedding or something was inscribed wrong or whatever."

"And the watch was a present too? That explains why there wasn't any mention of John having a wife in the police report."

"What police report?"

Oh, boy. "The one I found when I broke into Sutter's office."

"Waitaminute! What?" Fiona pulled Byline to a stop right in the middle of Lake Shore. "You did a break-in? What happened to I hold the flashlight and you pick the lock? That's how we roll! How could you do a break-in without me?"

"It was a spontaneous occurrence and you're dating a cop."

"So we won't bring him with us."

"Yeah, well, I'm no romance expert but getting arrested by the boyfriend isn't the primrose path to happily ever after."

Fiona flicked the reins. "So we don't get caught. Problem solved."

My guess was that Finn didn't tell Fiona all the nitty-gritty about Sutter undercover and Dead John because he wanted to keep her out of harm's way. I got that, even admired it. He suspected I was involved because I dialed his number. Also Sutter told him I was a total pain meaning I'd be in the mix somewhere.

"Hey, look at me." Fiona jabbed me in the ribs snapping me back to the moment. "What are you thinking? We're gal pals, together through thick and thin, wherever that takes us. There's no more thinking without me, right?" She stopped the carriage in front of Rudy's Rides.

"Right," I said, crossing my fingers behind my back. "It's you and me. All we know for sure is that John and Bladen were friends and Bladen gave John some presents. It doesn't make sense that Bladen had anything to do with John's murder, meaning Bladen's off the hook."

"And that puts us right back to square one?"

"Pretty much." But not really. Bladen and John knew each other and they knew Sutter. Sutter had the same knife as John so that tied the three of them - Sutter, John and Bladen - together and it led straight back to the undercover gig. John was looking for the guy in his wallet, making it a party of four. Did picture guy run off with the money? Did he find John first and knock him off because he was getting too close? Was Sutter next like Finn suspected? Whoever this picture guy was, he played into all this big time. I needed that picture.

I could have Finn get it but then Sutter would know I was involved. That would lead to another butt-out lecture and Sutter might tell Finn to go home. I needed Finn. This was getting a little hairy and I was no Xena Warrior Princess, though I bet I could really rock the outfit.

"You're thinking again, I can tell," Fiona grumbled. "There're little rings of smoke curling from your ears."

I gave Fiona a hug. "See you at the Stang, girlfriend."

"Can't wait for you to meet Finn. So, why did you leave the Stang so early last night?"

"Got a phone number off a bathroom wall." I held Fiona a little tighter and rushed on with, "Sounds like Finn really cares for you."

"Yep, I think he does and the feeling's mutual and getting more mutual every day."

By noon my workbench looked like a tornado had struck. The bride and groom bikes were finished, we'd rented out half our stock - thank you, Lord - and Cal was off to musket/cannon duty at the fort. We didn't talk about Fiona. We didn't have time with all the customers, but in any case a broken heart didn't mend overnight.

So that I didn't wind up with scurvy or rickets or whatever you got from carb overload, I popped a veggie burger in the nuker and gulped down a spoonful of foul-smelling tuna to satisfy some dietary requirement I read about on Facebook. I dumped the rest of the tuna onto a plate for Bambino and Cleveland, told them they had the culinary palate of a goat, and pulled the tab on a can of diet Coke. A body can only stand so much healthy at one time without going into shock.

I bandaged the knee of a customer who took a spill on Tulips and Lighthouses, one of my fave creations, and gave the rider a free dinner at Goodfellows. The saying *you never forget how to ride a bike* was pure crap. People forgot all the time, although they refused to believe it because of the stupid saying. That's why they signed waivers, and that's why I gave them free dinners when they crashed.

With the midday lull in effect, I pulled out a sketchpad for some spit-balling of new bike ideas. "Maybe a fifties themed bike?" I said to Bambino and Cleveland, asleep on the pool table and not raising one brow at my great inspiration. "What if I put vinyl records, an ice cream soda, and a poodle skirt on the front fender? Everybody loves poodle skirts! Great idea, huh?" I showed them the drawings.

No response.

"A jukebox, Elvis, a red convertible, and blue suede shoes for the back fender? Real crowd pleaser, right?"

Nothing.

"If I add a pink fuzzy seat and pink and black streamers on the handlebars, the bike will be downright adorable. Don't you agree?"

Still nothing. B and C were a tough sell.

The shop bell tinkled and abandoned fiancé Curtis from over at the Metivier Inn shuffled in. He stopped by the Spring Garden bike, his eyes beady, shirt half open, and bowler bowtie sagging around his neck. "My fiancée would love this one. Well..." He clenched his fists, his jaw tightened. "Who knows what that woman likes now but it sure isn't me, blast her lying, cheating heart and I hope she rots in Walmart's bargain basement for all eternity!"

I wasn't sure if Walmart had a bargain basement, but I handed Curtis a bottle of water, wishing it were laced with Prozac. "You know, sometimes a good ride can make you feel much better about things. It kind of gets rid of all those pent up frustrations and the raging anger tearing up and down your spine. If you're a golfer I have the Arnold Palmer bike or if you fish there's Outdoor Angler next to—"

"I don't want a blasted bike!" Curtis yanked off his bowtie and threw it across the workbench, the cats chasing it like a toy. "I don't want to get calm! I want an attorney, blast it all. I want a good one! I was looking for Bloomfield, Attorney at Law. I took the walkway to the office around back but no one's there. The note on the door says *Be back by two*. It's ten after. Where in the blazes is he!"

"She and that's my mother. She's running a little late. With a client, no doubt."

Truth be told, she was lunching with Angelo and probably having a great dessert to wind things up. Although being her daughter, I really didn't want to think about the dessert part. Mother came to the island to start afresh, told everyone her name was Carman, switched out her Ann Taylor attire for Mae West, and started dating Angelo, a retired mob boss. Bloomfields never did anything half-assed.

"Is your mother any good as an attorney?" Curtis ran his hand through his thinning hair. "I need someone tough." He pounded the workbench, causing me and the paint cans to jump. "I got myself into a mess and signed a prenup that's going to cost me a bundle and make Ms. Hot-pants rich. I need a shark of a lawyer. I need a shark who eats other sharks."

"Well, two summers ago Father left Mother for a Parisian fan dancer and took up drinking wine and painting nudes on the Left Bank. Mother now owns the house in Chicago, the condo in Naples and the family shotgun and no one can find the fan dancer."

“Sold! I’ll go check if she’s back. I got to get this legal stuff settled.” Curtis took a few steps and turned back to me. “I’d appreciate you not mentioning any of this.”

“What happens at the bike shop stays at the bike shop.”

Hoping to minimize any potential carnage, I followed Curtis, engaging in harmless chitchat about the weather and fudge as we made our way up the brick walkway that led to Mother’s office. It was a white cottage with red awnings and red geraniums in the window boxes. Mother lived on the top floor with a balcony overlooking the lake. It was the perfect mother-daughter arrangement. Close but not too close, Haagen Dazs in the freezer, Hershey kisses in the refrigerator, Kentucky bourbon for when things went straight to hell, and I had an attorney on speed-dial.

Curtis went inside the office and I waited until Angelo came out. I hooked my arm through his. “So, how was lunch?”

Angelo had on a black polo and black pants, the outfit of choice for retired Detroit mob guys, if indeed they ever really retired. Angelo, his sister, and now nephew Luca had moved to the island when their Detroit family commandeered SeeFar, a cottage up on the East Bluff, from a guy who owed the Family a bundle in gambling debts. Angelo considered Mother a dish, treated her like a queen, and was just what Mother aka Carman needed after a Paris encounter of the feather kind. I put on my biggest toothy smile.

"Uh oh. Now what?" Angelo let out a resigned sigh.

"I need you to teach me now to pick a Yale lock, the heavy duty variety, and I need you to make it a crash course so I can figure out who killed the guy on the dock."

Chapter Seven

Angelo shook his head and added another sigh. "I knew your mother and I should have stayed for another glass of wine at Millie's."

"Did you get the whitefish chowder?" I asked Angelo.

"I always get the chowder. Where's this lock?"

"It might be best if you didn't know."

We stopped at the front door of the bike shop and Angelo ran his hand over his face, muttering something Italian that probably translated into *why me*. "If your mother finds out about this, she'll skin me alive. Why are you getting involved? Did you know the dead guy?"

"Dead guy not so much, but you and I know the head honcho at the police station and there's a chance whoever knocked off the dead guy is now gunning for Sutter. Have you heard anything about our irritating local cop going undercover in Detroit as a mob boss a few years back?"

Angelo gave me a *you're completely whacko* look. "Not going to happen, kid. Nate's no Paul Newman. He could never pass himself off as a mob anything."

"Paul Newman like in salad dressing? What does salad dressing have to do with any of this?"

That got me another muttered *why me* followed by, "Look, all I've heard from the Motor City contingent of the Family is that there's some funny business with expensive hooch, smuggling, and Canada."

"Al Capone and rum running."

"Reverse prohibition without Tommy guns. Canada's got stiff liquor taxes these days. A decent Chianti here goes for around twenty-five bucks and the same bottle in Canada is double. That's a hundred percent return on investment at retail, but better still, whoever's heading up the smuggling operation is doing bulk wholesale. He's got a plan that gets the goods past customs and that's not so easy these days."

"The dead guy on the dock had a champagne bottle clutched in his cold, dead hands. Do you think there's a connection?"

Angelo let out a slow whistle. "Somebody's sending a message to steer clear or else, you should take that real serious. Upsetting their smuggling applecart will not go over well. As for this lock you're talking about..." Angelo stroked his chin. "Could be a static six pin Yale euro, that's the lock of choice for the paranoid. With a regular pick set, every time you push a pin you'll lose two and have to keep going back to the beginning to reset. The six pin is no paperclip and credit card operation. I'm thinking it's a job for the DAMES."

"No time to call in friends. I need to get this done tonight."

"Kid, I live with these DAMES. The Defense Against Mechanism Entry Set is pick tools with attitude. I got a 'em stashed under the pot of white gardenias in my upstairs hallway." Angelo added a wink. "Need an extra hand? Always good to keep my skills up to speed. Like they say, use it or lose it."

"If things go south, Mother finagling one of us out of the slammer is enough drama to deal with. I'll be fine."

"Sounds like something to put on a tombstone, Evie Bloomfield." I watched Obi Wan Angelo cross Main Street and head for SeeFar. Because I'd risked life and limb to save Meatball —Angelo's beloved bulldog who definitely fit his name — from sixteen thundering hooves headed his way, Angelo figured he was in my debt. While the debt had been paid off long ago, these days Angelo helped me mostly because the less time Mother spent getting me out of a jam, the more time she'd spend with Angelo. Deep down I suspected that, for Angelo, there was pride in passing on a well-honed family craft to the next generation. My nefarious intentions were all for the good, of course, at least that's what I told myself every time I straightened two paper clips and set to work.

"I should have been a dentist," Mother panted as she stumbled into the bike shop two hours later. She rifled around under the workbench, yanked out a Coke - the real deal, none of that Zero stuff - popped the top, and slurped the whole thing in one giant gulp. Impressive!

"I take it undoing prenups isn't so easy."

"You know about that?"

"Curtis needed a confidant."

Mother plopped down on the stool and swiped the back of her hand across her lips as Bambino and Cleveland jumped into her lap, purring like a furnace on a freezing winter day. "Not that I can tell you one way or the other with that lawyer-client privilege thing in effect. What I can say is that the antique Tiffany lamp Angelo gave me is smashed on the floor and Lord knows how I'm going to get it back together."

"He trashed your stained-glass dragonfly lamp?"

"Along with my autographed picture of Adele and you know how I love Adele even if she does make me cry like a two year old with an ear ache. Signing an iron-clad contract that went into effect the moment Curtis slipped that big diamond on the love-of-his-life's finger was not the smartest move the man's ever made. That she did the horizontal hula with someone other than Curtis doesn't make a speck of difference legally."

Mother stared at the Coke can and hiccupped. "One can of caffeinated bubbles and I'm all mouth." She added a very un-lawyerlike burp. "Why is there a door lock on your workbench in the middle of all the bike stuff and is that a paint can with notes stuck to it?"

"Uh, the old lock sticks and I need an upgrade, the paint can's kind of colorful and I already knew what you told me about Curtis. You didn't give any of that client stuff away. He's not a happy camper?"

"Godzilla on a bad day, but not as scaly. I'll have a word with Nate tonight at Fiona's party about keeping an eye on Crazy Curtis. The man isn't himself at all. Or he is himself and that may not bode well for his round-heeled fiancée." Mother deposited the kits on the pool table next to their new fave bowtie toy thanks to Curtis' tantrum. She handed me the empty can to recycle and I handed her a lint roller to de-fur.

"You are coming tonight, right?" Mother rolled the sticky tube over her navy dress with an adorable red jacket.

I felt the DAMES heavy in the pocket of my capris. "I'll be a little late. I just need to... figure out the lock."

"What you need is a professional, daughter dear." Mother dropped the roller on the workbench and headed for the door. "But make it snappy. We're all dying to meet Finn, except maybe Cal. We all feel bad for Cal."

"Everyone knows about Cal and Fiona?"

"The only one who doesn't know about Cal and Fiona is Fiona, except now there's Fiona and Finn. I'm afraid Cal may have missed his chance." Mother gave me a hard look. "Just like some other person in this room who we all know and love shall remain nameless but needs a big wakeup call in the romance department."

Mother added a sassy grin then closed the door behind her. With more customers trotting in, I didn't have time to consider the missed chance comment that I'm sure was about Sutter and me. At one time maybe there was a chance for a Sutter and me, but lately it was more Sutter versus me.

At seven I closed up shop, pulled out the DAMES, and tried to make sense of the seven picks in the black pouch. I jabbed in the long skinny one then the hooky thing and dug around like Angelo showed me, feeling the pins inside slide up then fall back into place. When Angelo did it the pins stayed put and the lock opened like magic. No magic for me.

“I’m never going to get this,” I said to feline one and two staring at me with *you’re hopeless* glints in their eyes. I slid the picks in my pocket, pulled on my fleece, and trudged off for the police station.

A rainy mist settled over the island, giving the full moon an eerie yellow halo. The Mighty Mac Bridge connecting the Lower Peninsula with the Upper was totally socked in except for tiny pinpricks of light forming the outline. A foghorn echoed between the hills as fudgies meandered from shops to bars to restaurants. Clouds snaked off the lake, curling over the streets and sidewalks and around buildings.

I turned down Astor, the courthouse/police station just ahead with its cupola lost in the haze. “Hi,” I said to

Molly, moping at the desk and drawing little hearts on a speeding ticket pad since they weren't used for much else around here. "No Luca?"

"Would you believe he's persona non grata?" Molly sighed. "Just because I filed my bologna sandwich in the B drawer and faxed the museum a memo on using their facility to store horse excrement when it should have gone to the sanitation department, Nate got his boxers in a bind and said I'm too distracted when Luca's around. If you ask me, Nate's the one who needs to get distracted once in a while. He's a total grump these days."

Molly gave me a curious look. "What happened to you being his distraction? You'd be doing the whole island a big favor if you'd get on with it and why are you here two nights in a row? There are better places to be like the party over at the Stang with Frugal Fiona footing the bill. How in the heck did that ever happen?"

"She's in love."

"Aren't we all. At least we should be." I got another grouchy look followed by another sigh. "Night duty is sooooooo boring without Luca. The only thing happening at this hour is a few drunks from over at Horns Bar or someone falling off the pier trying to get cell phone reception or maybe a—"

"A missing dog!" Angelo yelped as he hobbled into the station, favoring his left leg and leaning heavily on a stick he'd obviously found on the ground. He plopped into the chair on the other side of desk and swiped perspiration that wasn't there from his forehead. "Mamma Mia! My Meatball's run off and I twisted my ankle going after him! You gotta help find him before he comes to a ruinous end."

Angelo stuck out his right foot. "And my lumbago, how can it be this bad. I hope the little rascal's headed back to SeeFar and now that I think about it." Angelo added a wink. "Luca's got a pot of fantastico spaghetti sauce simmering on the stove if you happen to stop by."

Molly's eyes widened and she licked her lips. "I love Luca's sauce."

"It's Bolognese with pork and beef and bacon. Bacon's the secret. And he's baking bread. Italian, all crusty on the outside and soft and warm on the inside. You know how that boy loves things soft and warm."

Molly grabbed a flashlight as big as her arm from the desk and said to Angelo, "Stay here and nurse your injury and answer the phones. If Nate calls tell him I can't leave a little dog running around in this fog all alone, but don't say anything about simmering spaghetti sauce."

She nodded to the desk. "There's the two-way radio. You can get me on that thing if you need me. Don't need me."

Humming and skipping, Molly closed the door behind her and I turned to Angelo. "Ruinous end? And have you ever said Mamma Mia before in your life?"

"Ruinous end was forty-two down on the *Times* crossword today and Rosetta had *Mamma Mia* playing when I left the house, so sue me."

"Do you even know what lumbago is?"

"I think that was fourteen across. This morning Luca brushed his teeth with sunscreen and ate Meatball's kibble as breakfast cereal. I figured Molly's brain was mush like Luca's and I could pull off a Roving Rover - that's grifter talk for lost dog decoy. What's more innocent than an old man who's lost his pooch?"

"Old? Innocent? You! Were the comics next to that crossword?"

Angelo leaned back in the desk chair. "Heard from a certain lawyer that you needed a professional to get things done tonight. I wore my black fedora and crepe sole shoes for the occasion. I'm ready for action, kid, so what's the caper?"

"B and E into a police station. You sure you want to get involved?"

"I got more experience getting out of police stations than in, but change is good. Spill it."

"What I need is a picture from the evidence closet in Sutter's office. I think it's the person who did in the guy on the dock and is gunning for Sutter because of that mob boss thing I told you about. Sutter is not about to ask any of us for help, so we just have to jump in. After midnight, Molly closes the office and sets the alarm and 911 calls get forwarded, not that there're many. I have no idea how to deal with an alarm system, so I'm here now."

Angelo pulled a deck of cards from his jacket pocket and started shuffling. "So we got ourselves a little situation," he said over the chatter of cards. "Nate's at the Stang for that party Fiona's throwing." Angelo did a fancy card fan across the desktop between the computer and the gilded picture of Luca with pink kissy lips smudging the glass. "If he calls here, one of us has to answer and give him the song and dance about Meatball lost and me all upset."

"You really think Sutter will buy that line?"

"Not a chance, but by the time he shows up you'll be gone with the picture and I'll be playing solitaire." Angelo stacked the cards in the middle of the desk and stood. "We'll work in shifts. I'll spring the locks then you get what you need and take off. The lost dog story's pretty shaky even if that little rascal's always getting out, but if you're here too Nate'll smell a rat for sure. A very cute rat, but he'll know something's up all the same." Angelo held out his hand. "It's show time, kid."

I handed Angelo the DAMES. "Just wondering, but have you bought any raffle tickets to be police chief for a day?"

Angelo grinned ear to ear. "Wrote a nice fat check. The Detroit family's gonna get a kick out of it when I win, I can tell you that. Me on the other side of the law will make for a terrific Christmas card photo, that's for sure."

Angelo took off down the hall humming something Puccini as I watched the wall clock tick away my life and resisted the urge to hum *March to the Gallows*. I answered a phone call about how to get to the library for the evening lecture — amazing what people called the cops for around here - and gnawed my fingernails to the quick as sweat trickled down my back and between my boobs. I sucked as a grifter.

"Your turn," Angelo said from behind, making me jump a foot and bite my finger hard enough to leave marks. He handed me a flashlight. "Keep the lights in the office off and doors closed in case we get visitors." He tossed me latex gloves. "Always clean up after yourself. Words of wisdom from grandpa Dominick who lived by the motto *everyone gets paid, no one gets hurt, no one gets caught*. I have to ask if Nate's office is always that neat? Looks like Sunday brunch at the Grand Hotel in there."

"We figure Martha Stewart's his long lost auntie or he got vaccinated with a boutonnière." I made a low bow to Angelo, honoring his talent with a lock pick, and headed for the office with the old floorboards creaking as I went. Maybe I should ask for crepe sole shoes for Christmas? Maybe I should stop breaking into police stations!

I slipped on the gloves, closed the office door behind me, clicked on the flashlight, and headed for the evidence closet. Shelves lined the wall, stacked with blue boxes arranged by date. John Bernard's was right in front. The closet was cramped, so I took the box to Sutter's desk and pulled off the lid to find sealed evidence bags and a brown envelope. I dumped out the envelope, scattering the knife, money clip, wallet, and watch across the desk. I took pictures of the swanky guy in the wallet and the date on the knife before dropping everything back in the envelope and closing the box. For a second I studied the guy in the photo. He wore a white dinner jacket with a red carnation and black-rimmed glasses. He looked very gentrified, but more posed than relaxed. Having his picture taken was not this guy's bag.

I put the box in the closet, reset the lock, closed the evidence closet door, and pulled off the latex gloves just as Angelo's booming voice carried from the front of the station. "Buona sera, Nate!" I clicked off the flashlight and froze. Dang! What happened to the phone ringing? What happened to giving Sutter the song and dance routine? Nate Sutter was here in the police station and I was here in his office and I had no idea how to *not* be here!

"Heard Meatball's gone missing." Sutter didn't sound one bit convinced. "Any idea where he is?"

Angelo chuckled. It was very convincing, as if he lied to the police all the time. Go figure. "I think he's sweet on that cute little Bichon over on Cadotte Street," Angelo rattled on. "He probably took off for a late night rendezvous."

"Or maybe you cooked up a rendezvous between Luca and Molly and Meatball is snuggled up in your bedroom watching reruns of the Westminster Dog Show?"

Angelo laughed. "Notte d'amore, my friend, a night for love. I'm just doing my part."

"Yeah, well, some of us have to work at night, so you need to go home and I need to get to my office. If you happen to see my sergeant, you might suggest she squeeze in a little police work around her love life."

Sutter and Angelo exchanged good-nights. I heard the front door close, followed by footsteps approaching. Sutter was headed for his office, heading for *me* and an unlocked door. Sutter always locked his office door so he would know someone was inside. Or... maybe with a little luck Sutter's version of *his office* was guy code for the bathroom and he'd walk on by?

I held my breath and said a little prayer to the gods of weak bladders as little dots of panic danced in front of my eyes. The doorknob turned, killing any hope of a guy code. I hunkered down so as not to be seen though the frosted glass.

Sutter opened the door, sandwiching me between it and the wall. Lights went on. Sutter didn't pause for a second as if the unlocked door thing didn't register. I peeked around the edge to Sutter entering the evidence closet. He came back out into the office with John Bernard's box. He set it on the desk, rifled though the contents just like I'd done earlier, and slid something in his pocket as a voice yelling, "I wan' Bladen Dowers 'rested, right now," echoed up the hallway.

"Where 'r the p'lice when you nee' 'em, huh?" Was that Curtis at the front of the police station? Sure sounded like Curtis plus enough booze to pickle his brain.

"Da guy in the black hat said this was the p'lice statio'." There was pounding on the desk followed by, "He said I shoul' go to the p'lice 'cause I wan' Bladen Powers 'rested right now, but I don't see no po'ice here nowhere!"

"And it's feeding time at Mackinac Zoo," Sutter muttered to himself. He charged out of the room calling, "I'm coming, I'm coming. Keep your shirt on, will ya'."

"What if I don' wanna keep my shirt on, huh. What if I wanna be buck nekid and run through the streets in my birfday suit, huh? I got rights, naked birfday rights, everybody's got naked birfday rights," Curtis laughed.

As Curtis carried on about being naked and getting Powers arrested, I wondered what Sutter wanted with John's stuff. Sutter was the one who put the evidence in the bags so what was the big deal now? I tiptoed over to the desk and the brown envelope and contents scattered across on the desktop. The knife was there, as well as the money clip, driver's license bag, and wallet, but the picture of Swanky Guy was gone.

Sutter told Curtis to go home and sleep it off. The front door closed and Sutter's footsteps thundered down the hall toward me. I scooted behind the door again as he rushed in. He scooped the items back into the envelope, dropped it in the box, and hauled the box to the closet, giving me seconds to sneak into the hall and get the heck out of here. I held my breath and did a quick step from behind the door as the loudest creak in all of North America reverberated through the silence like a cannon blast.

"Chicago? What the heck are you doing here," Sutter said from the closet doorway.

Chapter Eight

"L...Looking for you." In a stroke of genius, at least it was genius for me, I stepped further into the office, acting as if I'd just gotten there. I slapped an innocent smile on my face. "Everybody at the Stang is wondering where you are. Thought I'd pop over to see if everything's okay."

Sutter raked back his hair. "I got a drunk fiancé streaking down Main Street and a missing dog that's probably more about Angelo playing matchmaker. I'll be at the Stang as soon as Molly can fit her job into her wedding plans."

"I'm here, I'm here," Molly bellowed down the hall. Panting and eyes sparkling, she popped her head in the doorway and grinned, her smudged lipstick halfway up her nose.

"Looks like you found the Meatball, just not the dog variety," Sutter grumped with a hint of a smile sneaking through. "Is that spaghetti sauce on your chin?"

Molly swiped her face. "Best meatballs ever and not the canine variety. You two go to the party and I'll lock up around midnight like usual. Luca's going to meet me at the Stang and good grief, will you two just try and look as if you like each other when you're together? It's good for island morale. Folks got enough on their minds with a dead body and no explanation."

I glanced at Sutter. He glared at me, frowned and shook his head as we headed for the door and right past the picture of him frowning again. Someone needed to tie the guy to a chair and force-feed him reruns of *Seinfeld*. "One of these days you'll have to talk to me," I said as we sidestepped a carriage trotting towards us.

Sutter stopped in the middle of Astor and held my shoulders. With the fog closing in around us muffling sounds and lights and swallowing up people and horses, it seemed as if we were the only two people on the island. "Stay out of this, Evie. For once just mind your own business."

I jabbed my hands on my hips. "I can help. I already know you were undercover as a mob boss."

At least that got a smile.

"And," I went on, "that the guy who killed John is after you."

The smile vanished. "Go paint bikes and your nails and help Molly plan a wedding before she and Luca drive us all nuts. I mean it, Evie. Put your purple paperclips away and quit breaking into places where you shouldn't be. Let this go for your own good."

"If that mattered I would stop riding bikes and I wouldn't have come here in the first place."

"Sounds like a plan." Sutter continued on to the Stang and I followed at a slower pace. Sutter never called me Evie. I was Chicago and he was Sutter and that's the way we rolled. This time he was serious, really serious, and Sutter and I didn't do serious. We did getting in each other's way, peaceful coexistence, and maybe a little fun now and then...but this?The Stang was packed and loud. Free beer and eats tends to have that effect on island locals. Garth Brooks' *Friends in Low Places* blared from the yellow and green vintage jukebox. I wandered up to the bar and sat down beside Irma, her arm linked though Rudy's. Scooter slid a Bud Lite in front of me then hurried off to fill more glasses. When the bartender knew what you wanted before you asked, maybe it was time to switch to Coke.

"You look happy," I said to Irma over the din. "Good day at the fudge shop?"

"Good enough, especially for this time of year. Business is slowing up for sure." Beaming, Irma squeezed Rudy a little tighter. "But the best part is come December we won't be here freezing our buns off on this island like we usually do and worrying bout freezing pipes and shoveling snow off the roof. We are now officially snow birds."

Irma pulled a set of keys complete with a pink flamingo from her pocket and dangled them in the air. "We're heading south to the land of margaritas and flower shirts and joining the old fart migration to the surf and sun."

"A cruise?"

"A Winnebago!"

"Business must really be good. At the bike shop I can maybe afford the margarita part."

"What's good is Nate." Rudy nodded toward Sutter playing darts with Finn and Luca. Rudy kissed Irma on the cheek. "Nate gave us the Winnie. Said his ship came in and this was a belated wedding gift. Like he didn't do enough with decorating the bike shop for our wedding ceremony."

"It that was such a lovely event." Irma looked dreamy and clasped her hands to her chest. "He completely transformed the shop into a wedding wonderland and I have no idea how he did it. The only thing I can think of is he watched *My Big Fat Greek Wedding* when he had the flu in high school and it must have somehow rubbed off on him."

Some guys learned to knit, some took up gardening. Sutter had been known to redo flower arrangements and table settings as if on auto-pilot. We all just thought of it as his thing, an escape from jail cells and paperwork. But the big question tonight was where did Nate Sutter get

Winnebago kind of money? A bank loan? What did he use for collateral? Shakespeare? He was a great horse but not winning the Kentucky Derby great and Sutter's old Victorian over on Church Street would have *This Old House* doing the happy dance. How'd Sutter get so rich so fast? And what was this payout for? Cops didn't have payouts, they had paydays and mortgages.

I passed on the second beer and asked for a Coke just as Finn won the dart match. He pulled on the blue *Winner* t-shirt and Sutter and Luca reluctantly slid on white *Loser* shirts. Fiona waved to me over the crowd. "Evie, we need pictures of second place Nate. This never happens." She planted a kiss on Finn's cheek. "I want pictures of me with the winner."

I got Sheldon from my pocket and wound my way through tables and the meandering crowd as Fiona took horn-rimmed glasses off one of the waiters. She slid the glasses on Sutter saying maybe they would help him win the next match. Fiona looked great. That mani-pedi appointment must have included a complete makeover of understated makeup, including matte pink lipstick and fake eyelashes, plus a sleek New York haircut with auburn highlights.

I snapped some shots then made my way back to the bar. I reclaimed my seat, flipping through the pictures hoping at least one turned out without somebody's eyes closed and my heart stopped dead in my chest. I flipped back to the picture I'd taken of the guy from John's wallet then back to the ones of Fiona, Finn, and Sutter. Fiona and Finn looked like two people in love, Nate looked just like...

"Honey," Irma said putting her arm around me. "You're white as beer foam. Are you okay? What's on that phone that's got you so upset? You young people spend way too much time behind those screens. It'll make you all half-blind and totally ga-ga before you're forty."

I turned Sheldon off and kissed Irma on the cheek. "Congrats on the Winnie and you better remember to send lots of postcards so we can all have Winnie-envy. Bring me back an orange."

I headed for the door, flung it open and gulped in the fresh air to try and keep from passing out. Fingers shaking I turned on my phone and flipped through the pictures again, slowly this time. The guy in John's wallet had on a white jacket, Sutter had on the white *Loser* shirt. Both guys had dark rimmed glasses and scruff and an awkward stance. Wallet Guy had a blond-streaked ponytail and Sutter had short dark hair, but twenty minutes and a box of Lady Clairol would take care of the color and hair extensions and a glue gun would make the ponytail.

Sutter was Wallet Guy? Possibly? I flipped again. A really big possibly. If Sutter *was* the guy in the picture and John *was* looking for that guy because he ran off with the five million, did that mean Sutter took the money? Is that why Sutter took the picture? I was getting to close to the truth? Did Sutter kill John so he could keep the five mil?

Okay, this was crazy! This was me on black cloud overload trying to solve a murder. Sutter was not a thief. Sutter was definitely not a killer. All I had were tiny little photos on an outdated phone, a tired brain, and a boatload of imagination. But the thing is, if I'd jumped to this stupid wrong conclusion about Sutter, maybe someone else would and they would think he was a crook with the loot and a killer. I had to put this to rest.

First off, I had to know what the Detroit undercover operation was about and who was involved. It wasn't only John – there had to be others if all that money went missing. Sutter wouldn't keep personal info about his past at his office, so that meant a trip to his home. With Sutter at the party, there was no time like the present to snoop.

I crossed to Main Street as I zipped my fleece. The fog had started to lift, and a hint of that full moon causing everyone to go loopy peeked through the clouds that were now dancing across the sky. I turned right and headed for Church Street figuring it was about a thirty minute walk away, fifteen if I put my mind to it. I had no idea how long Sutter would be at the Stang so I took off in a run.

"Evie, me dear girl," Irish Donna said trotting up beside me in her buggy. "Why ever are ye out here working up a sweat when you need to be at Fiona's shindig?"

I stopped to catch my breath, cursing every Nutty Buddy I'd ever eaten. Irish Donna bent down from her perch, the gold shamrock she always wore around her neck catching the lamplight and her red curls framing her always happy face. "You need to be enjoying the moment 'cause we all know Fiona springing for drinks and eats is not likely to be repeating itself anytime this century. I'm parking Patty boy here and taking advantage of the situation myself for a bit. My guess is Shamus is already there and flirting up a storm with the girls like he does. The only reason I don't mind is that it keeps him energetic in the bedroom if you get my drift." Irish Donna laughed then held out her hand to me. "Climb on up, me dear."

"I need a ride but not to the Stang and I need you to not ask any questions. Can you do that?"

"Nothing better than a bit of late night intrigue." Green eyes sparking, Irish Donna sat back in her seat and pulled her green wool cloak to the side to make room for me. "And as luck would have it, I'm in need of a body to help deliver a wedding cake tomorrow up there to the fort and you not get paid for the experience. I guess the question is, can you do that?"

Still panting, I climbed into the carriage. "Deal. I'll get Rudy to mind the bike shop for a few hours."

Irish Donna slapped me on the back, jarring me clear through to the bone. She flicked the reins. "So where we be heading and why is it so important to be getting there in a hurry?"

"The where is the corner of Church Street and as for why, what happened to no questions?"

"That part was me being polite. Now that we got polite out of the way, I'm thinking and hoping the why is you going to Nate Sutter's house and planning a little late night surprise for the boy?"

"That's one way of putting it." Especially if he caught me.

Irish Donna added a sassy laugh. "And you and I both know ye can't be having me drive you right up to the front door of Nate's house with Mira Brindle watching with her telescope like she does. In five minutes there'd be no surprise and the whole town would be knowing about it." Irish Donna gave me a once over and shook her head. "Dearie, I be no Kardashian, but an old yellow jacket and messy hair in bad need of a trim is not the way to be winning over a man."

She pulled under the streetlight and handed me a bag as I climbed down. "These here be blueberry scones just baked for Mrs. Gilmore. She's been feeling a might poorly but you'll be needing them more than her. Nate Sutter's a man and with you looking like something the cat coughed up these here scones are the only hope you got of getting anywhere in the romance department tonight."

Irish Donna trotted off and since romancing Sutter was not on my list of things to do, I dug into the bag for a taste of pure heaven. I crunched my way though dry leaves piled across the sidewalk as night crickets chirping their last songs of autumn. The scent of wood burning fireplaces wafted though the air and an owl hooted off in the distance. For a second I remembered life in Chicago with cars, horns and lights everywhere. Chicago was fine but Mackinac was a million times better.

I slipped into the bushes to keep out of sight from the prying telescope. Gnarled apple tree branches drooped low over the back walkway of Sutter's house and I scooted under, catching a spider web in my hair. I screamed, swiped at my head like a woman possessed, tripped over a rock, and landed face down in the weeds, strewing blueberry scones everywhere. The whole island was falling in love and I got spider webs. If Nate Sutter wasn't guilty of something after all this I intended to beat him to a pulp.

I pushed myself up, wiped my muddy hands on my jeans, found one scone not too badly damaged, and applied the five-second rule of not all that dirty. Okay, it was probably twenty seconds, but when it came to scones, close enough. I tossed the ruined pastries in Sutter's garbage can and stuffed the good one in my pocket. I headed for the back porch.

The chief of police would lock windows and doors but I'd give them a go anyway since Plan B was climbing the spidery apple tree to the second floor and I didn't even want to think about that. Rotting porch boards sagged under my weight, making me rethink the bazillion calorie scone. I pushed up on the first window. It didn't budge, but the lock mechanism holding it in place was like the rest of the house... antiquated.

From my back pocket I pulled my one and only credit card that I used for emergency C and E, that being cash and entering. I wiggled the card between the upper and lower double-hung window casing and flipped the hook off the latch. Considering how easily I got in the house it was hard to imagine there being five million bucks lying around.

I pushed up the window and hoisted one foot over the sill then the other. I poked Sheldon's flashlight app and looked around. I knew this was the kitchen from a previous unannounced night visit to Sutter's house two years ago. That time it was to check on a cat. No doubt Winchester was still slinking around somewhere or maybe hiding behind all the boxes piled everywhere or the stacks of fresh lumber, slabs of wallboard, buckets of nails, unopened paint cans, shutters, and a really sweet cherry dining room table and chairs covered in plastic. There was everything in here but the kitchen sink. No wait, a really nice country kitchen sink leaned against the far wall just waiting to be installed.

Right here were all the supplies needed for a complete gut job to make the house a showpiece. My guess was the other rooms were packed with new furniture and fixtures as well. With the island's construction ban from April through October so Mackinac looked pristine and perfect to the fudgies, Sutter couldn't start work on the house until next month. But everything was sitting here ready and...

Did a shadow of something just slide past the door? I spun around to a low growl and two beady eyes. It wasn't Winchester, but a really ticked off mean, snarling, not one bit happy I was on his turf, dog. "Hi?"

I got another growl and this one was accompanied by a lot of teeth and slobber. Cujo lives.

"Okay, I get it, I know my being here looks really bad, but actually I stopped in for a good reason." I slowly backed up toward the window I'd come through hoping to get there in one piece. "I'm trying to get Sutter off the hook for something it looks like he's done but probably didn't do," I added in innocent nice little-girl voice, "and somebody might be after him and I'm trying to figure that out too so maybe you can let me out of here in one piece."

I eased back a few more steps and my back hit something solid, warm, and completely unmovable. Slowly I craned my neck around.

Chapter Nine

"Sutter?"

"What the heck are you doing here?"

"What the heck are *you* doing here?"

"I live here and at the moment I'm saving you from being doggie dinner."

"Holy freaking hell you have a gun!"

"I'm a cop, I have guns."

"Including the one you need to pick up at my shop and is that glitter on the handle?"

"Long story." Sutter opened the kitchen cabinet and put the gun next to a box of oatmeal. "For the record I didn't know it was you." He hunkered down. "Come here, Sunshine."

In an instant the snarling canine transformed into a happy, yipping pet complete with wagging tail and perky ears. He bounded over to Sutter and licked his face. "Sunshine? More like Diablo and since when do you have a dog?"

"Since Mrs. Freemont went to live with her daughter and two cats over on Mahoney."

I studied Sutter for a minute. "You're not yelling or frothing at the mouth that I'm here. You weren't sure it was me, but you're not surprised to see me either." I stepped back and folded my arms. "You knew I was in your office. You knew I'd show up here next."

Sutter gave Sunshine a final pat, stood up, and stepped closer, the tips of his boots touching my Nikes and the heat from his body warming me clear through the fleece. "I always lock my office door and yet it wasn't locked. Then you suddenly showed up in my office out of nowhere, the evidence bags in John's box were put back in a different order than when I stored them, and whatever you think you know you don't."

"Let's give that *don't know* part a little test drive. I know you're the guy John Bernard was looking for. It was your picture John was flashing around town and why you wore a white dinner jacket and had a blond ponytail has something to do with the undercover operation in Detroit though I can't imagine what. No mob boss would be caught dead in those clothes. John thought you ran off with a lot of money and the Winnebago present and the Home Depot annex here in your house seem to confirm that. Except I don't believe you stole money or that you'd kill John to keep him quiet. And I know the real killer is probably gunning for you and that somehow this is all tied to smuggling champagne into Canada but even Angelo can't figure that one out. Your turn."

"I got the money from Amazon."

"And here I've been ordering books and makeup."

Sutter swooped me up into his arms, completely taking my breath away. He smelled of spicy soap, fresh air, and a touch of danger. "I helped a Detroit finance guy change a tire on I-94 back in '06. He said he had a good feeling about Amazon stock and I should look into it. He was driving a Porsche 911 turbo and I had a rusted pickup. I figured he might be onto something."

Sutter strode to the back door, opened it, and stood me on the porch. "As for the rest of this, don't meddle in the affairs of dragons for you are crunchy and tasty with ketchup."

"What the heck does that mean?"

"It means I finally got your attention. You should butt out of police matters or I will throw you in jail, and I am not kidding, Evie Bloomfield. I'm not kidding at all."

I pulled five dollars from my fleece pocket and slapped it in Sutter's hand. "This is my chance to be police chief for a day and then I can lock *you* up. So what do you think about that?"

A slow grin spread across Sutter's face, his eyes dark as the night around us. "I think I look forward to it."

Then he kissed me. His lips were delicious, seductive, and completely intoxicating, like warm mulled wine on a cold winter night.

"I shouldn't have done that," Sutter said in a whisper.

"It's a full moon, these things happen."

"Even when they shouldn't." Sutter closed the door in my face. At least I think he did except I couldn't think straight. I felt dizzy and lightheaded, totally brain-scrambled and blistering hot all over.

Get a grip, Evie! He's just a man. Yeah, but a really yummy man. *That was not getting a grip!* Sutter had kissed me before, but not lately. Two weeks ago we were having coffee and talking about Lettie McDonald and Becky Whitehead eloping to Vegas and how we should throw them a party when they got back to the island and the next day he wouldn't return my calls. For sure this had to do with the Detroit undercover operation and Dead John. But what?

All I got tonight was Amazon, changing a tire, and getting eaten by a dragon. Sutter didn't say boo about who was after him or the undercover sting or the smuggling. Well, if Nate Sutter thought he could bamboozle me with a kiss he was dead wrong. Okay, sort of wrong. There was definitely some bamboozling going on.

I pounded on the door. "I hate you, Nate Sutter."

I didn't really hate him, but I was frustrated on so many levels like not knowing what was going on, what he had done as an undercover boss, and where the heck the two of us stood - or didn't stand. I kicked the rock I'd tripped over earlier, headed for the street, and pulled the scone from my pocket, not caring that it was loaded with fat and laced with yellow fleece fuzz.

No matter how crazy things were between us, Sutter needed help now. He'd helped me out on more than one occasion, so I figured I owed him, right? And there was the fact that he kissed me... whatever the heck that meant. Right now I was going with that it meant something and no way was I going to let Sutter get blown to smithereens without knowing what that something was.

At the crack of dawn, Sheldon's alarm buzzed. Bambino and Cleveland leaped from the dresser onto my head to get my attention and remind me it was breakfast time. Everything I had to get done today flooded into my brain. I pushed myself up to find Finn sitting at the end of my bed drinking coffee. He shoved a steaming mug and glazed doughnut in my hands and asked, "Have any luck finding the mystery man from John's wallet?"

Staring at the front of my pink nightshirt he added a grin and read, *"Pajamas and pancakes forever?"*

"My dream job. How'd you get in here and couldn't this wait 'til later?"

"A hide-a-key rock by the back steps is a really bad idea especially when it's the only rock around and if I wait till later that has you surrounded by customers. When you left the party early last night I suspected you were onto something. The good news is you don't snore. The bad news is your hair looks like you got struck by lightning."

I turned to the mirror over my dresser and stifled a scream by stuffing the doughnut in my mouth. "Well, for openers," I said around a mouthful and trying to forget my Einstein hair, "Sutter is the guy John was looking for and it's probably best I not tell you how I figured that out."

Finn's brows shot clear to his forehead. "John was looking for Nate?"

"The one and only." I swiped crumbs from my lips as B and C paced the bed then sat on my pillow. "My guess is that John knew Sutter from his undercover days and for some reason thought Sutter ran off with the loot."

I considered that for a second. "You know, what if the guy who actually ran off with the five million planted the idea that it was Sutter who has the loot. That way it got the heat off him and on Sutter."

"You're smarter than you look." Finn added a sly grin. "Especially right now. The killer lures John to the docks saying he has information about Sutter being the undercover cop they're looking for then kills John."

"And frames Sutter and somehow a smuggling operation plays into all this." I took a sip of coffee. "You don't seem surprised by the smuggling."

"The undercover operation in Detroit was smuggling champagne into Canada. Detroit is a stone's throw away from Windsor with a lot of small boat harbors and inlets dotting the shorelines on both sides. Border patrol can only cover so much territory. Twin-engine bowriders can make the run in an hour at night, dropping the booze off at new locations each time, especially if they know the waters."

"John's job description was coxswain. That means he knew how to drive a boat? And his code name was Leadfoot. He had a fast boat."

"John might be an ace at rum-running, or in this case champagne running, but I doubt if he's the ringleader. Nate's been on a spending spree lately so he looks like the money guy, making him the next target on the hit list. If the killer knocks off Nate, it'll look like a revenge killing and the money trail ends with him dead."

"And," I added trying to think like a crook, "if the new smuggling operation ends too that really makes it look like Nate was the guy in charge all along and the real killer goes off into the sunset to enjoy his ill-gotten gains that he's probably got stashed away in some offshore account. Framing Sutter ties up all those pesky loose ends."

"Those offshore accounts let a lot of bad guys get away scot-free." Finn arched his left brow. "You're pretty good at this criminal stuff for a bike shop girl."

"Due to my black cloud syndrome I've had more than my fair share of practice.

Finn finished off his coffee. "I'll keep close to Nate. He'll be at the fort most of the day to make sure the wedding of the century and blessed by the Governor goes off without a hitch. Not that anything will happen there with so many people around. I managed to finesse an invite by sending the bride a congratulatory bottle of champagne. I borrowed a coat and tie from Nate and I'm taking Fiona. She's really psyched."

"I'll be serving cake and not psyched at all. I'll cut you a big piece. Fiona loves wedding cake."

Finn dropped the key in my hand then headed for the steps, the back door closing as he left. I turned back to Bambino and Cleveland, neither napping but both looking distressed. Usually that look was reserved for an empty food bowl and the threat of imminent Armageddon. "I get it, you like Nate and you're worried. Yeah, me too."

I fed the kits, grabbed a shower, and tried to tame my hair so as not to frighten small children and big horses. I then bribed Mother to help me get the bride and groom bikes up Fort Street, also known as the hill from hell, to Fort Mackinac. We dropped the bikes at the entrance. With me sweating like a roasting pig and Mother picture perfect in navy slacks and red blouse, we headed for the Blarney Scone, the bribe part of the deal. The last of the yellow climbing roses cascaded over the fence and doorway. On the inside, pink and yellow linens and china teapots graced every table and something by Mozart hummed in the background.

"Do I dare ask ye how your night surprise visit with Nate turned out?" Irish Donna poured Breakfast Earl Grey into Spode cups with pink roses. She added a wink. "Did ye manage to get his attention?"

"You could say that." I stirred in two lumps of sugar as Mother added, "What visit? You? Nate? How'd I miss this?"

"Next time," Irish Donna said to Mother. "You need to be lending Evie here one of your fancy-dancy red lace Carman dresses to seal the deal, if you know what I mean. We're all thinking a little fancy-dancy might brighten Nate's mood and that would do us all a world of good. And," Donna said turning my way, "don't you be forgetting to help me with the wedding cake. Be here around two to load things up proper. Can't be getting there too early or all the buttercream icing will go sliding right off the cake."

Irish Donna strolled over to another table to pour tea and Mother selected her second peach mini tart from the silver two-tiered tray. My second was blueberry. Okay, it was my third, but the way I saw it, mini-tarts meant mini-calories.

"Late night visit?" Mother arched her left brow and took a dainty nibble with not one crumb daring to fall. "Do tell and why are you on wedding cake duty? If you're smart, and we know you are, get paid in buttercream icing and save me some."

I bit into my tart as a blueberry squeezed out the side, dribbling down my chin and leaving a blue trail on my blouse before plopping onto the pink napkin in my lap. Whatever neat gene Mother possessed it had not been passed on to me. I wiped my chin, plucked the berry, and popped it in my mouth. No blueberry left behind on my watch. "I went to Sutter's house to snoop and got nowhere, Irish Donna needs help with the cake delivery up at the fort, and have you heard anything about Sutter being undercover while in Detroit and involved in some smuggling operation?"

Mother stopped her tart midair and stared at me. "Detroit has their share of bad guys but Nate Sutter as one of them even undercover is absurd. He's not the type to pull that off at all."

"That's pretty much what Angelo said and threw in something about salad dressing that didn't make sense at all."

"Angelo! Oh dear, I almost forgot." Mother checked her watch. She put down her tart, retrieved her napkin, and stood. "The two of us are running up to Sault Ste. Marie and staying the night. One of these days Angelo and I plan to visit some of the other islands, they are all lovely." She kissed me on the cheek. "Ta, darling, and Carman's red lace dresses are yours any time you want. Nate's a keeper, try to remember that."

Mother sprinted out the yellow door, the little bell dinging as it closed. I paid the bill and headed for the bike shop. It wasn't yet nine and a chill hung in the air with bright blue skies and puffy clouds overhead. The early-bird fudgies were out doing breakfast and window shopping, and I spotted Petula standing beside a buggy talking to Otis in front of Doud's Market. Was she wearing two different shoes and was that a banker's clip holding her hair in a ponytail?

"But you have everything in this store," Petula wailed to Otis, who was wearing his official green Doud's Market apron and matching bowtie. "All I need are a measly hundred little old wine glasses." Eyes beady, she grabbed Otis by the apron and growled, "That's not so many."

"Only if you own a vineyard." Otis shoved the two large boxes he'd been holding at Petula. "Like I said, I have these two dozen as in twenty-four wine glasses. Period."

"What about water glasses, juice glasses, toddler sippy cups?"

Wide-eyed, Otis turned to me as I came up the sidewalk. "You wouldn't happen to have eighty or so wine glasses over at the bike shop for this lady, would you?" He pointed to Petula and gave me the *beware the crazy tourist* look. "Please say yes for all our sakes."

"We're more a water bottle and granola bar kind of operation, but the Mustang Lounge might help." I turned to Petula. It's on Astor and not open yet, but you can go around back, tap on the window, and ask for Scooter. The password is *I love micro-brewed beers* and you're in."

Petula flung her arms around me, knocking me backwards. "Bless your little northern heart! I persuaded Eileen and a few maids from the Metivier Inn looking to make a few extra bucks to help out, but to tell you the truth I don't know how this wedding is ever going to pull together at the last minute. Something's going on with Bladen and he's more scattered than ever, if that's possible, and Daniela is madder than a wet hen. Bladen makes all the money and I do all the work. I need a raise something terrible!"

Petula slung the boxes into the buggy as if she'd done a lot of slinging in her life. She climbed up beside the driver, gave herself a little shake and pointed a stiff finger. "Onward to the Mustang Lounge."
Dray, driver, and Petula trotted off at a fast clip and I turned to Otis. "I think she's losing it."

"And it's never coming back."

Otis helped a customer with a crying baby and I crossed to the bike shop. Customers were already lining up outside to pick out their bikes for the day. With the summer rush of kids and grandkids and demands for Batman, Spiderman, and Paw Patrol gone and those bikes now in the back of the shop, the attention was on bikes with themes for adults. Naming the bikes gave them a special personality and I was surprised how often returning customers asked for the bikes by name. Besides Bride and Groom, this year I'd added Garden Party, Gone Fishin', Hole in One, Drinks On Me, Sail Away, and Shop 'til You Drop.

Once I got the early bike rush out of the way I dove into straightening up the workbench. Rudy was minding the shop today and I didn't want him to see the place such a mess. Okay, I'd been busy, really busy, and there were other things on my mind like murder and mayhem, but a mess was a mess and even I, Pigpen Bloomfield, needed some order.

I put the screwdrivers, wrenches, sockets, and pliers on their hangers in the pegboard over the workbench and hung up hammers and snips. Jars of screws and bolts went to one side and the chili pepper red paint can plus notes went to the other side. The other paint cans and spare parts got stored alphabetically on the correct shelves, and the avocado green paint can that served as my cash register went under the workbench. I stood back, admired my pristine workbench, and took a pic with Sheldon since the workbench wasn't likely to stay this neat very long. I was pretty much a bike slob. With everything ship-shape for a change, I rewarded myself with a chocolate chip cookie that somehow turned into three cookies as the next flood of mid-morning customers wandered in.

I helped a customer push the three-wheeled Birds of a Feather out the door and when I came back inside Rudy was sitting at the nice, neat workbench with Bambino and Cleveland snuggled on his lap. He was smiling and looking at my sketches for the soda shop bike.

"I like it." He tapped the sketch. "Add Elvis's blue suede shoes and you got yourself a winner here."

"Your lap cats are on the fence about the whole idea."

"The only themes these two would like are Where's My Tuna and The Litter Needs Changing."

Rudy had on khaki Dockers and a red Mickey Mouse t-shirt. He pointed to his chest. "Irma and I are already getting our Florida on. We're doing Disney and Harry Potter and then Key West. Oprah has a house there and Irma's determined to bring her fudge from the shop."

Rudy stroked Bambino and Cleveland, who had once been his fur babies and were named after Mark Twain's cats. With Mackinac Island having a patriotic parade for every occasion imaginable, the locals dressed up as historical figures to participate. Fiona was Betsy Ross, I graduated to Martha Washington since the other Martha retired to Arizona, and Rudy nailed Mark Twain perfectly. Most of us only dressed up for the parades except for Mark Twain, who popped up every now and then at other times to add some color to the town. In my humble opinion it was Rudy's excuse to swill fine bourbon and smoke a cigar.

When Rudy married Irma, he moved in with her and together they ran the fudge shop. Many things taste great in fudge like walnuts, chocolate chips, and peanut butter - cat fur, not so much.

"You've really turned this place around," Rudy said to me while still petting the kits. "Before you landed here the shop was on its last legs and I had a busted one."

"Before I landed here, I lived in a fourth-floor walk-up with three college guys and a monkey for neighbors. The monkey was the best of the lot and-"

"Where is she?" Curtis growled as he burst through the door. He had a wild look in his eyes and his hair looked like it had been combed with an eggbeater. This was the other curse of a full moon. Some people fall in love and others go bat-crap crazy when that love didn't go as planned.

Curtis still wore the same suit from the engagement party, with coffee stains dribbled down the front of his once white shirt. He hadn't shaved or probably bathed at all in who knows how many days. "I need that lawyer lady to get things straightened out right now," Curtis added. "Katie, my floozy of a fiancée, is threatening to sue me for breach of contract when she's the one playing hide the salami with... with *you!*"

Curtis pointed to the front door and lunged for Bladen Powers as he strode into the shop.

Chapter Ten

"Me?" Bladen held up his hands in surrender and backed up to the door. "Who the heck are *you*?"

"You planned my freaking engagement party!" Curtis bellowed as Bladen darted behind a row of bikes for protection. "And as your bonus you slept with my fiancée."

"Katie?"

"How many fiancées have you slept with!"

"She was nervous about riding on the ferry."

"What ferry? You were already here at the inn and..." Curtis's eyes bulged. "You slept with her more than once?"

"She was really, really nervous."

"And you should be nervous too, you no good cheating piece of slime. 'Cause I'm going to settle the score right here and now." Curtis pushed over the line of bikes to get to Bladen when Rudy and I grabbed his arms before he landed a punch.

"Let me go!" Curtis struggled. "This ratfink has it coming."

"Ignoramus seems to be the name of choice," I offered to Curtis as Rudy and I hauled him to the stool by the workbench and sat him down. "And," I said, turning to Bladen while keeping a hold of Curtis who was a lot stronger than he looked, "You need to get out of here while you can. If you're hunting Petula, she's on a wine glass quest."

"Right, wine glasses. I forgot about the glasses." Bladen slapped his forehead with the palm of his hand. "I just wanted to thank you for the bride and groom bikes." Bladen added a sheepish grin then bolted out the door.

I got a bottle of water from under the workbench and handed it to Curtis. "You need to calm down before you rupture something. Your attorney is away for two days, but she'll be back in town on Monday and can handle all your legal needs at that time."

"Monday! Are you kidding me? I can't wait until Monday! I want action now, right this minute. Katie's leaving on the noon ferry and I want her arrested for fraud. She tricked me and I want her locked up and the key thrown into the blasted lake. I've had enough of just sitting around doing nothing. I can't eat, I can't sleep. I'm a mess."

"So, maybe you should rethink this." Rudy hunkered down beside Curtis.

"You're right. Brilliant idea! I should hire a hitman."

"Not what I had in mind," Rudy soothed. "It's like Mark Twain said, anger is an acid that can do more harm to the vessel in which it's stored than to anything on which it is poured. Write this woman off and let this whole thing go. Get on with your life."

Little blood vessels throbbed at Curtis's temples and his eyes looked like roadmaps. "Screw Twain. Screw you! Do you know how much money's involved here?" Curtis gripped the plastic water bottle shooting water out the top like an angry volcano and doused Rudy from head to toe.

"But think of this, things could be worse," I said to Curtis as I handed Rudy the roll of paper towels to dry off. "You could have married Katie."

"There is no worse. I look like a total fool. My dad warned me about her being a conniving gold digger, so did my uncle and my brother and my ex and she's just going to love being right again. Another thing I'll never hear the end of. Well, Katie's gone, but Bladen's still here and why that police chief can't arrest him for sexual harassment is beyond me. Bladen messed up my wedding..."

Curtis stopped ranting then added a laugh that sent shivers up my spine. "But now I think I've got a plan, a big plan, to mess up his life. 'Bout time Romeo got a taste of his own medicine and I'm just the guy to do it."

Curtis bolted for the door, flung it open, barging into customers on their way in. Rudy dried his face and soggy mustache. "You know that saying about a woman scorned?" He ran a towel through his bushy, Twain-inspired hair. "It goes double for a rich guy made to look the fool."

Leaving Rudy to deal with customers, I righted the bikes and tried to shake off the bad vibes I got from Curtis. He had that wild look in his eyes, the look that promised trouble. If there was on thing we did not need more of around here it was trouble.

I rushed upstairs to try to find clothes suitable for serving wedding cake. I pulled out the curling iron and fried my hair into submission, winding up with a Shirley Temple/Marge Simpson 'do without the blue. As for clothes, I considered pink polka dots the perfect outfit for serving cake, but in keeping with the wedding attire I hunted for black slacks. I found a pair in the back of the closet that I could squeeze into if I left the top button undone and added an untucked white blouse to cover the gap.

"'Bout time you be getting yourself here," Irish Donna tsked when I rushed up to the delivery wagon parked outside the Blarney Scone. "Ye be looking like a French poodle with all those curls."

"Rudy says I look adorable."

"Rudy's wanting cake and buttering you up to get it."

"And about that cake," I pushed on. "You know Daniela will strangle us with her bare hands if something happened to it, so that makes this cake delivery a matter of life and death and we should call the ambulance to take the cake to the fort. Right?"

Wrong. It took a nerve-racking half hour of Irish Donna driving the wagon with me in the back, trying to keep cake layers from sliding into cake soup. As we trotted along, I thought about getting Irish Donna to keep an eye on Sutter, but then I'd have to tell her why. Then the whole town would know why, putting everyone in danger. If the killer found out we were all onto him, he would go into hiding and we would never find him...or her. Besides, like Finn said, what could happen with so many people around.

Irish Donna avoided Fort Street and the main entrance flanked with the white limestone walls and wood posts. She headed for the more level back entrance though the Avenue of the Flags. Each flag leading to the fort and fluttering in the breeze represented a country that had owned the island at one time. Everyone at the Stang thought they needed to add a flag with a slab of fudge to represent the current occupants.

Once inside the fort, we clip-clopped past the cream and brown soldiers' barracks and across the grassy parade ground. I waved to Cal in his blue uniform calling out orders to the other soldiers practicing a drill and none of them looking too happy about marching around in the hot sun.

"It seems Daniela's wanting the cake served up there on the cannon platform overlooking the town," Irish Donna called back to me from her driver's perch. She pulled a paper from her dress pocket and read, "The order of the day from her majesty is that the bride arrives through the Avenue of the Flags with soldiers forming an arch with their muskets, not that a certain someone has a mighty big opinion of her ego-inflated self. Cocktails at the quartermaster's house, and then ceremony on the front porch of the soldier's barracks followed by the firing of the muskets. Those things might be old as the hills, but they do cut up a ruckus even when just shooting off black powder like they do and always scaring me half to death."

Donna pulled Paddy to a stop and continued reading, "There'll be tables on the parade ground for dinner followed by cannon firing at the gun platform. I think the woman's got a thing for artillery. She and Cuddle Cakes...does anyone know the man's real name...cut the cake and then carriages take everyone on a sunset drive to the Grand Hotel for a night of dancing. Sounds like a USO show if you're asking me."

I hopped from the back of the wagon and Donna pointed to the cake layers. "Let's put Mariah Carey in the fort commissary so she won't melt all over and before you go making a thing of it I name all my wedding cakes just like you be naming your bikes. This here cake we have today is top heavy and hard to work with so Mariah Carey fits and to prove my point here comes the bride right now."

"Where in the blazes are the tables?" Daniela shrieked, charging up to the wagon. She wore short shorts, a pink t-shirt with *Bling, Bling, I Got the Ring,* her hair in fat blue curlers, and a big red zit on her nose.

I tried not to zit-stare as Irish Donna climbed down from the wagon and draped an arm around Daniela. "Dearie, there's no need to be carrying on the way you are," Donna cooed. "We have a cake table right here with us along with lovely china dessert plates and pretty pink linens and-"

"Not that!" Daniela jabbed her finger at the parade ground. "That! Where are the tables and the chairs? I heard Bladen was buying up every basket and blanket in town for a picnic wedding and I rushed right over here."

Her brows narrowed. "Those baskets and blankets he's collecting better not be for my wedding and I'm here to make sure of it. I'm serving Cornish game hens for Pete's sake and... where's the bunting on the porch for the wedding ceremony? The flowers and candle stands are there, but no bows, no ribbons, no zing. I bet they're still over there in the schoolhouse. My wedding's looking like a freaking wake. And where are the doves to be released when Cuddle Cakes and I say I do and kiss? I want kisses! I want doves!"

"What about seagulls," I offered. "We have a lot of seagulls. We could put out some fish to entice them except that might smell and-"

"See this?" Daniela jabbed a finger at her nose. "See that zit?"

"What zit?" Irish Donna gave me a *don't poke the bear* look and added, "I don't see anything."

"It's the size of Montana! I knew that romp in the hay with Bladen wasn't worth having him as my wedding planner, but I did it anyway 'cause he's so handsome and Cuddle Cakes might be from the New Hampshire Combstocks and of good breeding but he isn't all that proficient in the bedroom if you know what I mean." She swooshed back her hair. "It was one last fling and truly sublime and..." Daniela cut her eyes from me to Irish Donna and shrugged. "Just keep that last part to yourself if you want to get paid."

Daniela shoved a rectangular white lace box at Donna. "Here's the knife to cut the cake." She pried up the lid to a lovely engraved antique silver cake knife and...and a silver-plated antique derringer?

Daniela grabbed the little gun and shoved it in her pocket. "The knife was my great, great - I forget how many greats - grandmother's. She used it at the fort and I'm donating it to the museum. If those chairs and tables don't materialize real soon," she hissed, "I intend to use this donation in my pocket to get Bladen's attention and take me seriously. Have you seen that worm slithering around?"

"Maybe you could just threaten him with a bad Yelp review?" I suggested. Donna added, "And since you're into donations, if you make a monetary one to the fort here I bet that cop standing next to the flagpole will do your bunting. No one bunts up a wedding like our chief of police. You should see what he can do with a staple gun and bolt of ribbon."

Daniela offered up one last harrumph. "Well, he wasn't much use in getting Fort Road closed for my wedding pictures, but I guess it's worth a try." Daniela stomped off for the flagpole just as Finn came across the parade grounds heading for the soldier's barracks. If someone were hunting Sutter, Finn had his back and it made me feel a lot better to know that I wasn't the only one on Sutter alert. Not only were four eyes better than two, but Finn would know what to do if the killer made his move and it would be better than my plan to tackle him to the ground and beat him over the head with a cake knife.

Donna and I carried the cake layers to the commissary and pulled out the serving table. We propped up the legs and set the table by the wall with the glorious Mackinac Bridge off to the right and the town below bathed in golden afternoon sunlight. Peaceful deep-blue water stretched out as far as I could see. It was a picture-perfect afternoon. At least the weather and view were cooperating or Daniela would be crabbing at them too.

"Mercy be, is that there Bladen sneaking in through the main gate?" Donna nodded over the edge of the wall. "And are those baskets and bags slung over his arm? If Daniela is still here this is not going to be pretty."

"So," I said to Bladen coming our way. "The picnic idea is for real?"

Bladen swiped perspiration from his forehead nearly poking himself in the eye with the baskets on his arm. "Fall weddings are in demand and there were no tables left to rent, so I came up with this great picnic idea."

Irish Donna fluffed the pink tablecloth. "Heading to Mexico with no forwarding address is what I would call a great idea."

"Think of the photo opps on Facebook and Twitter!" Bladen forced a grin. "Think of the uniqueness."

"Think of Daniela blowing your head clean off your shoulders and you might want to take that to heart."

"After the wedding ceremony," Bladen went on, "every couple gets a basket with an official Mackinac Island blanket to commemorate the occasion. They find a spot on the parade ground and get served there. Pretty cool, huh?" Bladen dropped the baskets in a heap and pulled a navy blue throw with I ♥ Mackinac Island in white from a shopping bag. "And we'll add a bottle of chardonnay and we're putting glasses in the baskets. Some are beer mugs, but they hold more wine so it's just fine."

Bladen nodded to the post headquarters. "Petula and her crew that she's overpaying with my money are putting the baskets together right now. They'll line up the baskets by the barracks and who's that doing the bunting on the barracks porch?"

"That be our police chief." Donna held up a pink napkin. "He showed me how to fold these into swans."

Bladen stared at Sutter tying puffy white bows to the porch railings. "It's... It's the Benjamin Bow."

"Actually that be the Nate Sutter Bow. The other man who doesn't know tulle from toothpaste and is reading the newspaper is Fiona's latest fling. The way things are going between 'em you can be planning her wedding here next."

"John said he was closing in on Benjamin Campbell," Bladen continued as if talking to himself. "No one ties bows like Campbell. I think he patented the things. It must be him but it sure doesn't look like him. Where's the blond ponytail? Campbell really rocked the ponytail, but this guy kind of looks like him and those are his bows... It is him!"

Bladen strode off across the parade ground. He dodged the soldiers marching in two columns of five each and didn't slow down until he got to Sutter. I got that John and Bladen were looking for the guy in the picture who just happened to be ponytailed Sutter and who they thought ran off with the loot. So ponytail Nate Sutter was Benjamin Campbell? He was the mob boss who tied pretty bows? Tony Soprano never tied pretty bows unless they were around bodies tossed into the East River. None of this made one bit of sense. Who the heck was Benjamin Campbell and what was his part in all this?

I watched as Bladen pushed Sutter, yelled something I couldn't hear as Finn stepped between them and tried to calm him down. Donna nudged my arm. "We need to get a move on. If this here wedding has any chance of working out you better quit your gawking and get these baskets to Petula. Here's hoping Bladen contacted the caterers about turning their fancy little chickens into a Colonel Sanders affair."

Sutter went back to tying up the last of the bows and Bladen stomped his way to the quartermaster's house yelling something about this not being over. Bladen passed under the line of trees and I started down the wood walkway as practice musket blasts echoed across the parade ground. Irish Donna was right, real or not they scared me half to death too. Rounding the corner I spotted Bladen sitting on the steps of the post headquarters. He was hunched over staring at the ground, the bag of blankets in a heap at his feet.

"Hey, it's going to be okay," I said in my best Pollyanna voice to try to put a positive spin on things. I'd had my share of hunched over staring days and they weren't fun "I think the picnic idea is great," I lied but for a good cause. "And the Mackinac Island throws are really nice keepsakes and... and... Bladen?

I gave his shoulder a little shake. "Hey, are you okay? Look, this wedding isn't worth having a stroke over. Just pull yourself together and we'll all pitch in and help and..."

Bladen teetered for a second then tumbled off the steps head first landing on top of the blankets and leaving a trail of blood in his wake.

Chapter Eleven

"Bladen!" I dropped the baskets, knelt down and turned him over to find eyes frozen open and a blood-soaked shirt. Daniela ran up beside me, let out a scream straight from *Psycho*, and crumbled into a heap.

"What's going on?" Petula asked. She stopped, stared, and fainted next to Daniela as Eileen from the Metivier Inn said, "Guess I wasn't the only one really pissed off at that guy."

Irish Donna peered over my shoulder. "Blessed St. Patrick. I send you to deliver a few baskets and look what happens."

Sutter ran up with the entire militia thundering behind him as a worker in a brown shirt tore for the back entrance to get help. Sutter hunkered down next to me and said to Cal, "Looks like a stray musket round."

Cal shook his head and tried to help Daniela sit up. “No way. With all the tourists the insurance company won’t let us keep any live ammo anywhere near this fort.”

“I...I didn’t think it was loaded.” Daniela steadied herself and leaned against the wheel of Cal’s chair. She held up the little silver derringer with two fingers.

Everyone stepped back and Sutter took the gun. “Why would it be loaded?”

“I fired it last night for fun, but I didn’t think there were bullets left in the other barrel. I sort of forgot there were two barrels. I just wanted to scare him a little and when he fell down I figured I scared him a lot.”

Color returned to Daniela’s cheeks. “All I wanted were tables and chairs. Somebody on this freaking island has got to have some tables and chairs and I needed Bladen to think I meant business so I pulled out the gun and maybe I happened to squeeze the trigger and don’t look at me like that, these are desperate times.”

Daniela swiped a strand of hair from her forehead and squared her shoulders. “Guess my wedding planner’s not going to be much help now. I swear the man can't do anything right."

Sutter looked a little dumbfounded. Considering he was once an undercover mob boss, that was saying something. "You don't shoot people over tables and chairs."

"Let's go with the heat of the moment and an unfortunate accident that wasn't planned."

"Let's go with involuntary manslaughter."

"I like my idea better." Daniela stood and dusted herself off. "But right now I need to get dressed. I think my zit is getting smaller and is that the aroma of roasting game hens wafting my way? That means the caterer is on the way and all systems are a go."

Sutter stood. "Are you serious?"

"Absolutely. Game hens are my favorite."

"Look, you can't get married here. This is a crime scene."

"Oh my goodness, you are so right. What was I thinking?" Daniela pushed up the sleeves on her shirt. "We need to do something with this body. I'll get the feet, some of you men grab the arms, and we can drag Bladen into the post headquarters. We'll cover him up with those god-awful blankets he bought and throw a few over all this messy blood. Why in the world are you all just sitting there looking at me like I've got two heads. There's work to be done. Let's get a move on, people. Tick tock."

"I bet some brides really do want to kill their wedding planners," Scooter said as I hauled my tired self up onto a stool at the end of the crowded bar, "but death by musket ball is a little over the top. So, did you take an arm or a leg?" Scooter slid a beer in front of me as the jukebox blared a very inappropriate *Bang, Bang, My Baby Shot Me Down*.

"Doc Prichard took Bladen to the medical center in the ambulance," I said, trying to ignore the fact that this probably had something to do with my black cloud. "Sutter took a totally pissed off Daniela to jail, the caterers and I took the food to a homeless shelter on the mainland, and Irish Donna and Petula took Mariah Carey here." I nodded at the lovely wedding cake with the first two layers half eaten. "Wedding cake without having to cough up a wedding present is a pretty sweet deal. No wonder business is good tonight."

Scooter added a plate of fried green beans next to my beer. "Business is good because we're all wondering how to camouflage another murder so the fudgies don't stampede for the docks and the island goes bankrupt. A dead dockworker can be chalked up to a rough way of life, but Bladen was a wedding planner bumped off in broad daylight at a major tourist attraction. How do we get away with that one?"

I took a sip of beer. "Daniela and friends are billing this as a fort malfunction that happened after hours, whatever that is, to avoid further embarrassment. But if anyone else croaks we'll need an emergency town council meeting to come up with more lies. I think we're fresh out."

"Or we can just go with the truth for a change." Sutter reached over my shoulder, grabbed my beer and gulped half the glass. "Bladen's demise was an accident and not caused by Daniela and really was a fort malfunction of sorts."

Sutter snagged two fried green beans and plopped them in his mouth. "Fact is," he said between licking his fingers, "Daniela's getting married as we speak on the front porch of the Grand Hotel, new wedding cake and all, proving that money can indeed buy happiness. Doc said Bladen was killed with a musket ball and not a 41 rimfire which is the ammo in Daniela's derringer, meaning she's off the hook. Some of the reenactors use their guns for hunting and one of them must have forgotten they had a live ball loaded. When they did a practice firing, Bladen was in the wrong place at the wrong time. None of the reenactors knew Bladen so there's no motive and no way of knowing which musket the ball came from."

"So it's classified as an accident?" I asked.

"Not exactly." Finn walked up and put his hand on Sutter's shoulder. "We got a problem, Houston, a big one.

Nate Sutter," Finn said in an official cop voice, "you're under arrest for the murder of Bladen Powers. We found your gun."

Everyone in the bar froze, Scooter pulled the plug on the jukebox, and the place went dead quiet. Sutter did a slow turn to face Finn. "What are you talking about? Bladen was shot with a musket ball. I have two Glocks, my first BB gun, and granddad's World War II revolver."

Finn held up an evidence bag with the 1812 flintlock Sutter had gotten as an award. "One of the reenactors was cleaning up and it fell out of a wad of tulle in the schoolhouse at the fort. It's been fired recently, Nate. Molly told me to take a long walk off a short pier when I said she should bring you in for questioning so that's why I'm here. What the heck's going on?"

Sutter's brows knit together. "I forgot the pistol at the Grand Hotel two nights ago and haven't seen it since. Do you really think I'd be stupid enough to leave a murder weapon at the scene of the crime?"

Finn did a slow headshake. "You were at the fort for the wedding, nobody else was tying bows, and it would be easy enough for you to come back later and get it when investigating the crime scene. You knew Bladen and John from your undercover days and they thought you ran off with a lot of money so they were out to get you."

"So I got them first? I didn't take that money.""Expensive presents, new digs." Finn added.

"Investments."

"To launder the cash. And you are smart enough to use the flintlock to shoot a musket ball and pass it off as a wayward shot from one of the muskets during a drill. You know the fort, you know the soldiers hunt with their muskets, and you know how to get away with murder. This is the way the district attorney will play it. Except..."

Finn ran his hand through his hair and closed his eyes for a second. "Except I know you're not a killer. Everyone in this room knows this is a frame job. But unless something happens right now to keep you out of jail so you can prove yourself innocent, I'll have to arrest you."

Finn gazed around the room. “Does everyone understand what I’m saying?”

We all exchanged looks, nodded, and then accidentally on purpose I fell against the cake table. Mariah Carry swayed like a high-rise in an earthquake then tumbled over onto Finn, plastering his chest with buttercream rosettes, delicious goo, and a bride and groom figurine perched on his shoulder.

“Oh my goodness, how in the world did that happen?” I jumped in front of Finn, swiping at the mess across his front. The crowd parted like Moses and the Red Sea and Sutter bolted for the door. The crowed closed ranks as if nothing happened and Finn asked, “Where’d Nate go?”

“Nate who?” Scooter plugged in the jukebox and handed Finn a mug of beer. “It’s my latest small batch brew. I didn’t know what to call it, but now I’m going with The Great Escape. Let me know what you think.”

Everyone went back to what looked like drinking and eating and darting as usual but underneath the place buzzed about Sutter. From what I could tell the odds were twenty-to-one in Sutter's favor. I plucked the bride and groom figure off Finn's shoulder and licked icing from the bottom. "Now what do we do?" I asked Finn around a mouthful.

"Now we find out who really killed Bladen and John and is trying to pin it on Nate and why. Any idea where he'll hide out? We need to talk."

I stuck the bride and groom in Finn's pocket, their little heads peeking out over the top. "You've jeopardized your job and integrity enough with this latest charade." Fearing a buttercream overdose, I resisted the urge to pluck a rosette from Finn's collar. "You don't need to add aiding and abetting a fugitive. Besides, I have no idea where Sutter is."

Finn gave me a half grin. "You really suck at lying."

"Yeah, but this time I'm telling the truth and at least I'm not the one covered in wedding cake." I gave Finn a kiss on the cheek and headed for the door. I pushed it open to life as usual except for the resident chief of police on the lam. Lovers walked hand-in-hand, a Mission Resort taxi trotted past making a final night trip back to the hotel, and Fiona ran my way.

"What happened now?" She huffed when we met up under the streetlight. "I saw Nate tear out of the Stang like his pants were on fire and he didn't stop or even say hi. Did he figure out who killed Bladen?"

"Yes and no." I pulled Fiona into the alley beside the bar and lowered my voice. "Bladen was shot with the pistol Sutter got as an award."

Fiona's jaw dropped. "Get out of town."

"Why the heck couldn't they have given Sutter a blasted plaque like every other committee around here? But no, it had to be a flipping gun that actually worked and now he's really in a mess. One of the reenactors found the pistol at the fort, it was recently fired, Sutter knew John and Bladen from the bad old days in Detroit, the motive being Sutter stole money. Finn came in to arrest Sutter, and then Finn sort of let Sutter slip away."

"That's my man. Always doing the right thing, and he knows Sutter is innocent. So, why is there buttercream icing on your fleece?"

"Let's just say you'll want to eat Finn up with a spoon in more ways than usual. We need to talk to Sutter. Nearly everyone on the island would hide him except he won't go that route. He wouldn't put anyone in harm's way with the killer out there, and he wouldn't want to get someone in trouble with the law. My guess is he's headed for a place out of the way."

"Girlfriend, it's an eight-mile island, there is no out of the way. Nate's tucked in somewhere for the night. Maybe the Grand Hotel stables or the butterfly house or the back room at Doud's Market between cases of potato chips and Campbell's chicken noodle soup. Who would want to knock off Bladen and frame Sutter for it?"

Fiona shook her head. "I got nothing and it's been a long day. You got the cats to feed and I've got Finn, but you need got to cross your heart and pinky-swear you won't do anything on your own. The killer's out there and like you said before, another body won't matter to him or her one little bit."

Fiona took my thumb and crossed it over my heart and circled my pinky with hers. "Breaking a cross-heart pinky swear along with your black cloud will have you growing facial hair by morning and all your teeth will fall out. For all our sakes, go home."

Fiona hugged me then headed for the front door of the Stang. I started for the bike shop then made a detour for the police station.

Molly wouldn't arrest Sutter, but she might know the best hideouts for fugitive cops. This wasn't exactly sleuthing on my own and risking facial hair. It was more of a fact-finding mission, right? Here's the thing, I needed to talk to Sutter by myself. Molly took an oath to uphold the law and bring in the bad guys and Finn-the-cop did the same. Getting Fiona involved would complicate her relationship with Finn and they were really happy together. I wanted it to stay that way.

I turned right onto Market. The outside light to the police station/courthouse stayed on all night, but the inside of the building was dark meaning Molly had already locked up. Not that I could blame her with Luca McYummy waiting. I hurried on past the closed doors then slowed and stared at the side windows. Was that the swish of a flashlight darting around inside the police station? I knew that swish since I'd done it myself a time or two.

But who would break into a police station other than me? Bad guys wanted out not in. Except this may not be a bad guy. Where was the very last place anyone would ever think to look for a fugitive? And this particular fugitive knew how to disarm the alarm system.

Chapter Twelve

"Okay, Sutter, where the heck are you?" I whispered into the darkness of the police station after using my trusty purple paperclips to get in the back door. The red Exit sign glowed above and a faint thread of outside lamplight angled its way into the hall, offering little in the way of visibility.

"In the cell. What are you doing here?"

"The sight of you behind bars in your own jail is worth the price of admission. *Ouch.*"

"Watch the corner."

"I would watch it if I could see it."

I felt along the wall until I got to iron bars and then an opening. I shuffled inside the cell, feeling the empty air until I touched Sutter's forehead, strong chin that needed a shave, slightly crooked nose from one too many police encounters, and lips that had kissed mine not nearly enough. Where did that last part come from? From being alone in the dark with a man... this man.

My eyes started to adjust to the dark and Sutter took my hand and pulled me down beside him onto the bed. "Anyone see you come in?"

"You're talking to the queen of subterfuge. This mattress is really comfy."

"Serta Perfect Sleeper." His shoulder brushed mine. "Only the best for Mackinac criminals that consist mostly of bar fight refugees and BRWIs, better known as Bike Riding While Intoxicated. You smell like vanilla." He leaned back against the wall and exhaled a tired sigh.

"Don't use your phone flashlight, the rays bounce off the walls and are visible from outside. That's how I knew you were here. So," I leaned back against the wall next to Sutter, suddenly tired to the bone. "Got any idea who wants John and Bladen dead and wants to frame a once-upon-a-time prissy mob boss for the deed?"

Sutter grinned, his teeth white against the night. "Not sure how the mob boss thing got started. I was undercover alright but as a — okay, you're really going to love this one - wedding planner."

"Very funny."

That got me a half-smile and a wink. "My gun fell into a tub of glitter glue and fixing floral arrangements and buffets got to be knee-jerk reaction."

"Your serious?"

"You think I'd make that up?"

"Well dang. That explains a lot, the bows, the flowers, why your desktop is neat and desk drawers a mess. No one looks underneath the glitz."

"How do you know about my desk drawers?"

"Lucky guess. So a wedding planner because there are a bunch of brides and grooms robbing banks and knocking off liquor stores these days?"

"Because brides and grooms order a lot of expensive liquor and wedding planners are in the perfect position to over order and smuggle the excess into Canada, especially with Windsor only a short, fast boat ride to Detroit."

Sutter massaged the back of his neck, his shoulder brushing mine again. “The Canadian and US border patrols on the Detroit River knew something was going on, but the pickup and drop off locations for the boats changed each time. After a month of bow/flower/tulle/garter/party training I got hired on as a wedding planner by Wedding Wonderland because they thought something fishy was going on. Before that the only tulle I knew was of the screwdriver and hammer variety. Anyway, I wormed my way into the operation and got a tipoff that ended up being an ambush. I’d blown my cover, caught a bullet in the leg, and used a garter I had in my pocket to stop the bleeding.”

“There wasn’t enough evidence to nail anyone,” Sutter went on. “Finn sent me back here to recuperate and lay low. I was the obvious one to have run off with the money. They knew I was a cop and that I knew the lake. My guess is that John asked around about me while working on the freighters and told Bladen, thinking that together they’d get me to give them the money or they’d rat me out as a crooked cop. I think Bladen must have been the brains behind this all along and knocked off John so he could keep the money."

"Except now Bladen's dead. So who's really behind this?"

"That's just it, I still keep coming up with Bladen. He knew the wedding business, how to fudge orders, and he knew John, who had a crew. What if John and Bladen's murders aren't connected?"

"Curtis was after him for sleeping with his fiancée."

"And Curtis threatened me with legal action for not arresting Bladen. Eileen Fisher wanted me to arrest Bladen for breach of contract. He promised her she could be his assistant and all he wanted was a roll in the hay. But murdering someone over a job?"

"And being two-timed. Bladen was doing the deed with her too. She threatened Bladen with a hedge trimmer and a haircut is not what she had in mind. And she was at the fort," I added starting to put the pieces together. "Anyone could have taken the pistol from my workbench and the whole town knew the reenactors were practicing for the wedding. I gotta say that knocking off Bladen with your pistol with the same ammo was really clever. I need to pick up Nancy Drew at the Metivier Inn tomorrow and I can chat it up with Eileen. Before you launch into a lecture about staying out of trouble, I ruined a perfectly delicious cake to save your butt so... Sutter?"

I looked over at Sutter. His eyes were closed, breathing slow and steady, head tilted slightly to the side. Taking his shoulders I tipped him over onto the pillow, hauled his legs up onto the bed, and covered him with a blanket, no doubt from Pottery Barn. I took the cell phone from his hand. There was a callous on his thumb and more across his palm; his skin was rough. It was a workman's hand. He was a man who got the job done no matter what and I liked him a lot. And he was in a ton of trouble. It was one thing to come up with ideas on who might be the killer, it was another to prove it and we were a long, long way from that.

I bit my bottom lip and felt a tear slide down my cheek. I held Sutter's hand a little tighter. "I've lucked out two times finding the bad guy," I whispered into the darkness, “and if anybody up there is listening, not that I deserve anyone to listen but if you are, I’d really appreciate your help one more time. Please, let me nail one more bad guy and I’ll turn in my flashlight and paperclips and be content with painting bikes and eating junk food.” I made a cross over my heart and meant it. “Promise.”

I wiped away another tear and set Sutter’s cell phone alarm for five AM. It was still dark at that hour so he could sneak off. Molly would be in the station around six and maybe Finn too to lend her a hand. I didn’t think they would keep Sutter in jail, but it wasn’t fair to again make them choose between friendship and the law.

I kissed Sutter on the forehead then tiptoed out of the jail.

“You really don’t think the murders are connected?” Cal said to me early the next morning as we sat at the workbench. “Both guys were from Detroit, they knew each other and Nate, and they were all involved in the smuggling operation."

I handed Cal a cup of coffee. "Bladen has extenuating circumstances. At least three people were royally pissed at him." I counted on my fingers. "He ruined Daniela's wedding, double crossed Eileen, and slept with Curtis's fiancée. All of them blamed Sutter for not stepping in and arresting Bladen. Daniela's off the hook, so that leaves Eileen and Curtis."

Cal ran his hand over his Marine buzzed non-hair. "Except for her bad taste in men, Eileen's no dumb chick. I sat behind her in algebra and she let me copy. I sucked at algebra. Curtis is CEO of his own hat company, Hats by Hathaway to Top Off Your Day or something like that. Anyway, I bought him a beer at the Stang and he gave me tips on using LinkedIn to get good employees for the island. I'd say he and Eileen have the smarts to steal the pistol, shoot Bladen during a musket drill, and frame Nate."

"Eileen didn't shed a tear over Bladen toes up and eyes open, but I can't just say, *Freeze! You're under arrest*!

Maybe I should bring her a chocolate cream cheese muffin from Martha's Sweet Shop. A nice sugar high could get her talking. What do you think?"

"I think you want a cream cheese muffin. Did you ever consider eating oatmeal for breakfast?"

Morning sunlight glistened off the tall spires of the Mackinac Bridge and dew still clung to the trees that had turned from summer green into autumn wow. There was always a line at Martha's at eight AM, but it gave me a few minutes to appreciate the morning sounds of shopkeepers opening their doors, hanging baskets overflowing with mums of every hue swaying in the breeze, kayakers heading out into the lake, and cleaner-up Karl giving the streets a final sweep with his trusty broom and trash can on wheels to start the Mackinac Island day afresh.

"Hear anything from Nate?" Bonnie asked as she handed me my pink bag across the glass display case of all things yum.

"Nothing. I just hope he stays out of sight. He's no good to anyone behind bars."

"So maybe he's walking behind something else, something big and kind of smelly. He is a man of many talents, some we never knew he had."

"I don't get it."

"Oh, good grief. Just ask Karl to keep an eye out for Nate." Bonnie went on to the next customer and I headed outside and did a double take at the resident street sweeper.

The island had an automated street cleaner pulled by horses that did a really good job of keeping the streets tidy, but Karl was an institution around here, a local figure keeping the place perfect, or as near perfect as horse travel would allow. Except today Karl looked different. Taller, maybe? With his hat pulled low on his forehead.

"You missed a spot," I said as I crossed the street, pausing in the middle. "And where's Karl?"

"Having a root canal and I'm filling in. He got the better end of this deal I can tell you that."

"So you're going with the hiding in plain sight plan?"

"Better than Doud's freezer. I dreamed I got attacked by tater tots."

"And you really had a ponytail?"

"Catch up with you later, Kemo Sabe."

"Shower first. You'll scare the cats." I continued across Main Street then cut up Astor to Market.

The Metivier Inn in was picture perfect Mackinac Island. The quaint Victorian hotel was the stuff postcards and TripAdvisor used to lure fudgies here. Nancy Drew was probably parked around back where I dropped her off, but right now I wanted to see Eileen. I took the front steps to the wrap-around porch with hanging ferns, wicker rockers, and guests sipping coffee, Italian roast no doubt. Eileen dropped off a tray of pastries and started back inside as I asked, "Got a minute?" I held up the pink Martha's bag, making it do a dance in the air. "Even the help gets a ten minute coffee break, right?"

Eileen hitched her head toward the back of the porch and hummed *Walking on Sunshine*. I followed her down the steps to the side yard and a stone bench. She snatched the bag out of my hand, grabbed a muffin, and landed a bite that would do Jaws proud.

"I'm starving," she said around a mouthful. "Being in a good mood always makes me hungry. Bladen finally got a bit of his own, though I gotta say, death by firing squad is a bit much even for an ignoramus."

I grabbed back the bag and got the other muffin before Eileen gobbled them both. "And to top it all off Sutter didn't arrest Bladen for leading you on," I mumbled around a mouthful of crumbs, "so that had to make you double mad. I suppose he got what he deserved too."

I gave Eileen a meaningful look over the top of my muffin and added a nonchalant shrug, trying and keep things casual while accusing her of murder.

Eileen stopped mid-chew and swallowed. "You... you think I knocked off Bladen?"

"And framed Sutter for the deed. Well done, you."

"For your information I just happened to be with someone when Bladen was knocked off. And when I say *with* I mean like in the biblical sense not that I can tell you who my alibi is ’cause it wouldn’t be good for him. And another thing, Missy.” Eileen stood and brushed muffin bits from her pink apron. “Just because you got the hots for Nate Sutter and we all know it, don’t go trying to pin Bladen’s demise on me to clear Sutter.”

Eileen tossed her hair. “In fact, I think Nate Sutter’s guilty of doing in that John guy and Bladen. From what I’ve heard Sutter stole a lot of money when he was in Detroit and it caught up with him. How else could Nate afford giving Irma and Rudy that Winnebago? Not on a cop’s salary, that’s for sure.”

“He had investments. That’s how he got the money and Sutter is not a killer or a thief.”

“Yeah, that’s what all the guilty ones say. I watch NCIS, I know how these things work.” Eileen snagged my half-eaten muffin right out of my hand and marched back to the porch.

“Well, that didn’t go so well,” Petula said from behind me. She had on a floral dress and tan jacket with perfect makeup and her hair pinned up in a nice 'do. "But take my word for it, Eileen's not your killer."

"What happened to you? You look great."

"It's really what happened to Mr. All-Play-and-No-Work Bladen Powers." Petula flashed a toothy grin that benefited from recently used Crest whitening strips. "I don't wish him harm, but since he got it anyway, things have turned out right peachy. You're looking at the new senior wedding planner for Wedding Wonderland. I sprang into action and got Daniela married up there at the Grand. Daniela tweeted, Facebooked, and Instagrammed all over the place about how the Grand Hotel came to her rescue and how wonderful I was to pull it off."

Petula fanned a check in my face. "And I convinced Curtis to pay the bill for his engagement party. He'd refused before saying Bladen was the reason he lost his fiancée but now he's happy as a pig in mud. Bladen Power's demise might not be so good for Bladen Powers, but everyone else around here is all giggles and smiles."

Petula gave me a little finger wave and strolled off and I thought about the giggles and smiles. She was right, Bladen dead made her day, made Eileen happy, and put Curtis in a good mood and all that had to lead somewhere. But right now I needed to get Nancy back to the shop before the morning rush and Cal got swamped with customers.

I found Nancy parked by the back door. I was never going to get better at riding a bike if I didn't practice. With it being early and traffic light, now was the perfect time to give Nancy a go, right?

"Holy cannoli, what happened to you?" Cal asked as I limped into the shop with my ripped jacket flung over the handlebars. "I'm guessing it has to do with Nancy Drew looking like she got run over by a steamroller but since we don't have steamrollers here..."

"I sort of crashed into a dray. No harm came to any horses unless you count uproarious side-splitting laughter followed by equine snickering."

“Good thing you didn’t have on a Rudy’s Rides t-shirt. Talk about bad publicity.”

“I feel so much better now.”

“And I think you killed your jacket.”

I sat on the stool and grabbed the first aid kit from under the workbench. I kept it there for clumsy customers. Who was I kidding? I mostly used it on my clumsy self.

“Let me patch you up,” Cal said as he rolled my way. “Then I have to get back to the office. I have two employees lined up for Jack’s Livery and need to see if they know one end of a horse from the other. Did you get any info out of Eileen?”

“She was with someone when Bladen got shot and I believe her. Go do your interviews. I’m fine and you can patch up Nancy later.”

Cal rolled toward the door and stopped. “Do you think Fiona’s happy with Finn?”

I suddenly wished the dray had run me over and I was any place but here answering Cal's question. "Yeah, I think she is."

Cal gave me a tightlipped nod. "Good. That's what I want more than anything."

Cal opened the door and left as two customers entered. They looked at me and a mangled Nancy Drew then turned around and exited in a hurry. "Yeah," I said to Bambino and Cleveland sitting on the workbench, "it's going to be one of those days and I'd appreciate a little sympathy for a change. And since I feed you and shelter you and you don't do laundry or vacuum around here, I think it would be nice if you guys got me a doughnut with sprinkles to cheer me up. So there."

I stored Nancy in the back so as not to frighten off any more customers then I duct tapes the rips on my jacket. It looked like it had been mended by an orangutan, but I pulled it on anyway to hide my elbow Band-Aids. With Cover Girl's help I hid the scrapes on my nose and chin. With holey jeans being the in style, I was good to go as another wave of customers descended.

"Lord have mercy," Mother said, barging in the front door with four customers staring at her wide-eyed. Her hair was more bird nest than lawyer sleek and was that a spot on her navy jacket? Did the earth just tilt on its axis?

"I'm gone one night. Just one, mind you," Mother carried on, "and all hell breaks loose around here and why are you wearing makeup? You never wear makeup and why is your jacket held together by tape? Crime on a cupcake, what's happened around here?"

I flashed the customers a friendly grin and gestured around the shop. "Choose any bike you like and it's on the house. Just have it back by tomorrow." I snagged Mother by the elbow and hauled her outside to the porch then into the side walkway that led to her office. "Who squealed?"

"There was a note in Angelo's fridge thanking him for the salami and provolone sandwich along with a bottle of Chianti. It was signed The Fugitive. Luca filled us in on the details and I see a scrape on your chin and nose. You really need to give up biking, dear. Maybe you should put that on a t-shirt so you remember."

"Sutter's on the lam and accused of two murders and we have to find the killer and you're an attorney and I can't talk to you about any of this in case..." I swallowed hard. "In case Sutter's brought to trial. You can't lie and I don't want you to have to give evidence against him. I, on the other hand—"

"Will lie and get tossed in jail because you suck at it." Mother put her arm around me. "Is it that bad?"

"Most around here like Sutter, but some think he's guilty of taking money when he was in Detroit and that he knocked off Bladen and the guy on the docks to keep it. I'm afraid that if someone finds him they'll turn him in and you know what happens to cops in prison. I'm running out of time and suspects. The island is just not that big for Sutter to say hidden. This morning he doubled as a pooper scooper."

Mother added a tight grin then it faded completely, her blue eyes nearly black with concern. "Look for the person who has the most to gain. That part's harder than you think. It's not clear until you start digging around and that can get very dangerous very fast."

Mother took my hand. “I’ll see what I can find out on my end. If you need help call me. I might be a lawyer, but that be damned, I’m your mamma first.” She added a sassy shrug. “Your proud mamma.” She kissed me on the cheek then headed down the path to her office.

I’d probably lost some sales, but when your mother says she’s proud of you, especially when you thought you were the black sheep of the family, that was worth all the money in the world. Tired and sore I doused the lights in the shop except for the neon green bike light that hung in the window. I hobbled up the stairs to grab a shower and nearly collided with Sutter coming out of my bathroom shrouded in a towel, a really little towel. “You’re...you’re naked.”

“You’re early.” Sutter tried to rearrange the towel that was a regular sized towel, at least I thought it was, but truth be told Sutter didn’t have much material to work with.

“You keep the shop open until eight,” Sutter added, “and why are you smiling?”

"I'm not smiling and what about eight?"

"That's when you close. It's only six now so I thought I'd be gone when you got home. You're the one who told me to get a shower."

"Not here!"

"What happened to your nose and chin?"

"It was the horses' fault." I darted into my bedroom and came back with my robe. "It's big and it's fluffy."

"It's Hello Kitty."

"Everybody's a critic." Scooting past Sutter I grabbed his clothes from the bathroom counter. "I'll wash these before my house smells like Mackinac on a bad day and I'll make you something to eat and—"

There was a knock at the back door and I said to Sutter, "Don't panic, its just Mother. She's trying to find out what's going on in the legal world about you so maybe she's come up with something."

I raced down the stairs as fast as skinned knees would allow. I headed for the kitchen and my closet with the stackable washer and dryer and spotted Finn and some mean-looking guy in a cop uniform standing at my back window staring straight at me.

Chapter Thirteen

The cop yanked opened the door and strode inside just as the hall steps creaked and my heart stopped dead in my chest. I said in a loud shaky voice, "Finn, who's your big police friend here? Nice uniform?"

"This is Sergeant Abrams from Detroit. He's here to help Molly since she's short-handed."

"And to hunt down Nate Sutter because Molly won't?" I folded my arms to bunch up Sutter's clothes into an unrecognizable bundle.

"Someone else in the house with you?" Abrams grumbled. "And what's that smell?"

"What smell?" Abrams was clean-shaven, with beady eyes and a continuous unibrow. He was built like a tank and had about as much personality.

"Thought I heard someone on the steps." Abrams added.

"Cats." I looked from snarling, bristle-tailed Bambino and Cleveland standing on the kitchen windowsill to Finn doing a very slight shake of his head warning me off. "Lots of cats," I pushed on. "In fact we're having a cat sleepover."

"Anyone ever tell you that you're a terrible liar."

"If I had a nickel."

"Anyone ever tell you it's a crime to lie to the police."

"Anyone ever tell it's a crime to arrest the wrong person."

"Get out of my way." Abrams pushed me aside making me drop Sutter's clothes and scattering them across the floor as Finn said, "Now wait a minute."

From the corner of my eye I saw Sutter start down the steps as Cleveland and Bambino, in a flash of black and calico, leaped into the air landing claws-out on Abrams' chest while Mother barged into the kitchen wedging herself between Abrams and me. "Gotawarrant?"

"Get 'em off me! Get 'em off me!" Abrams roared, his arms flailing as he stumbled backwards. I tucked Bambino under one arm, Cleveland under the other, and kicked the clothes under the kitchen table while Abrams roared again. "You're making things worse, lady."

"Lawyer lady to you," Mother said getting right up in Abrams' face while I positioned myself in front of the clothes. "Touch my daughter again and you'll see what worse is all about."

"Come on," Finn said to Abrams and opened the door. "We're not getting anywhere here."

Abrams gazed down at his front. "I'm...I'm bleeding."

"Tell the local police how you were scratched by a cat," I seethed. "That should impress the heck out of them."

Abrams slammed his hand on my kitchen table, scaring the heck out of me, thinking he'd seen the pants and shirt under it. Instead he stormed out the door and Finn followed, glancing back at Mother with a quick nod and a little smile.

“Thanks,” I said to Mother. I put the kits back on their perch and grabbed a can of tuna. “I’m so sorry you had to get in the middle of all that.” I dumped the tuna onto saucers for the feline heroes. “I put you in a bad spot.”

Mother grinned ear to ear and fluffed her hair. “Dear daughter, this is an attorney’s idea of a day at Disneyland. Now you just go about doing your laundry and anything else you happen to be doing, but do it out of sight. There’s this thing called exigent circumstances where if the police see a suspected felon, they can go after him no warrant needed.” Mother twirled around and strutted out the door.

“Well done,” Sutter said from the steps.

“Yeah.” I pulled in a deep breath to get my heart rate out of the danger zone. “Carman aka Ann Louise Bloomfield is the best.”

“I was talking about you.”

I turned to Sutter. His eyes were dark, his hair still wet from the shower, and the Hello Kitty robe was exposing some mighty fine chest hair. I knew for sure there had never been a more handsome man and with the police breathing down our necks, this was not the time to do anything about it. "Abrams will be back, won't he?"

"Yeah. He'll call some judge and he'll get his warrant. You're on thin ice, Chicago, all because of me and things are not going to play well for Finn either. He's bound to catch a lot of flack for letting me get away."

I dumped the clothes in the washer and added extra detergent and some lavender fabric softener I got in mail. These clothes needed all the help they could get. "You mean my cake ruse didn't ring true?" I pulled out the skillet and set it on the stove.

"Probably doing great on YouTube, but in the land of law and order we're screwed. So, did you find out anything from Eileen?" Sutter sat on the third step and Bambino and Cleveland snuggled together on the bottom step with their favorite new toy bunched between them. "And when did you start wearing bowties?" Sutter picked up the mangled swath of material.

"Curtis left it and the kits took it over. Better than a squeaky mouse, especially at three in the morning when I step on it. As for Eileen, she has an alibi."

I got eggs, bacon, and cheese from the fridge and popped bread in the toaster. "She was getting it on with some guy and won't say who because it will get him in trouble."

"Meaning he's married."

I lined the skillet with the bacon and cracked four eggs in a bowl. "But beyond that," I added while whisking, something that always made me feel like a real cook though I was anything but. "I don't think she killed Bladen. She's seems too happy to go around shooting people."

"Unless she's happy because she shot him."

"It was like a content blissful happy more than a *yippee I did it* happy." I flipped the bacon. "Next on the who did in Bladen list was Curtis, but he wasn't at the fort to that rules him out, and then there's Petula, Bladen's assistant. She was royally ticked that Bladen wasn't paying attention to wedding details, but killing him over flowers and cake and risking prison over tables and chairs is a stretch. Got any suggestions?"

I looked back to Sutter, turning the mangled bowtie over and over in his hand while he was thinking. "Curtis was at the fort. I only saw him from the back and at the time I didn't know it was him. I caught a glimpse of his shirt."

Sutter held up the bowtie. "The shirt was this same pattern. I mean how many guys around here have bowler hats on their shirts and ties?"

"A brown shirt, right? Yeah, I saw him too. He ducked behind the quartermaster's house and I figured he was getting help."

"Except Doc never mentioned someone coming to get him. Cal called Doc on the landline inside the Visitors' Center and your bacon's burning."

"Oh, it's more like Curtis' bacon is burning. This is really good news." I scooped the slabs onto a plate, blotted with a paper towel to get the grease then dumped the eggs into the pan. I tossed in a handful of cheese.

"There was no reason for Curtis to be at the fort other than to hunt Bladen. Curtis wasn't the one getting married and I doubt if he even knew Daniela."

"And Bladen caused Curtis a lot of grief and money and Curtis was mad at me."

I gave the eggs a flip. "I think we got ourselves a viable suspect, Sherlock." I slid the eggs onto the bacon plate, added the toast and handed it to Sutter. "I saw Petula, who looked a lot more like a wedding planner than a frumpy assistant today. She said that Curtis was in a good mood, even paid off the outstanding bill for his ruined engagement party. I need to find out what's got Curtis doing the happy dance, like maybe Bladen dead as landed mackerel."

"Be cool and don't tip your hand that you're onto him. If you get something, find Finn." Sutter held up the plate. "Don't you want some of this?"

This? I considered what was under Hello Kitty. Holy freaking...! "Loaded question." I handed Sutter a fork and ran out the door.

I hurried down Main Street to closing shops, nightlife taking over from fudge-hunting tourists, and twinkle lights adding a fairytale quality. I tried to push all thoughts of Naked Nate out of my brain and think about where Curtis could be at this time of night.

"Evie?" Fiona huffed as she ran up to me. "Are you ignoring me or what? Seems like all I do is run after you these days. I called to you three times and you didn't even slow down, girl. I told you not to go sleuthing around without me and I know that's what you're up to. Did your hair and teeth fall out? Have you seen Nate?"

"Not as much of him as I wanted to and hair and teeth are still attached. I have a lot on my mind."

"Like buying a new jacket? Duct tape? Really?"

"Duct tape is in and as for the killer, I think I might be onto something. I thought Eileen, a maid over at the Metivier Inn might have done in Bladen, but she was enjoyably occupied at the time though she won't say who."

"She could be lying, you know. Killers tend to do that."

"Except she had the same twinkle in her eyes and flushed glow as you do and probably for the same reason. Anyway, this Curtis guy was at the fort when Bladen was shot and Bladen slept with his fiancée causing a seriously expensive end to the wedding. I'm trying to find him and have a chat."

Fiona hooked her arm though mine. "So tonight we're on a manhunt? Since I'm free as a bird you can consider me your wingman. There's this horrid cop from Detroit—"

"Abrams. We've met."

"And he's following Finn around. Now we have no time together at all. The sooner you and I nail the real killer, the sooner I get my man back. I say we start with the Pink Pony. Bars are the perfect place to find a jilted male licking his wounds."

We walked into the Pony with its mural of dancing pink horses and a guitarist strumming out *Sweet Caroline.* Tourists in North Face fleeces sat at the bar swilling local Michigan brews and taking selfies. Some rougher types in green *Barefoot Gal* windbreakers occupied a table in the back cluttered with bottles of Bud. I turned to Fiona. "He's not here."

"Never fear." We headed for the door. "This island may have a ton of fudge shops but you and I know there are even more bars. We're just getting started."

Fiona and I crossed Main to Horn's Bar, finding pretty much the same scene as at the Pony. Then we headed for the Seabiscuit that was equal parts good booze and good food.

"There," I said as we came in the front door with Seabiscuit the racing wonder horse stenciled on the glass in case anyone forgot Mackinac Island was crazy about horses. I nodded at a guy alone in a booth having a lobster BLT, side of onion rings, and a brew.

"Hi," I said sliding into the bench across from Curtis with Fiona pulling in next to me. "So, how are you doing? Looks like you got your appetite back."

"And then some." Curtis patted his belly that could do with a little gym time. "All thanks to your mother. She's negotiating a buy-out with Katie-the-tramp also known as my ex-fiancée." Curtis wiped his mouth and took a gulp of beer. "And the guy she was tramping around with is at present occupying space at what passes for a morgue on this island. If you ask me all is right with the world."

"So now you're headed home?" Fiona said and snagged one of Curtis's onion rings.

"You know, the island is pretty great. Came here a lot as a kid and it's one of the reasons why I wanted to have my engagement party... Well, you get the idea. I hate having those good memories ruined, so I'm thinking of hanging around and making some new ones. My hotel is terrific and things are kind of looking up for me now."

"And you can celebrate the nice job you did on hiding the pistol you used to shoot Bladen and framing Nate Sutter for the deed." I snagged an onion ring and held it up in salute. "Congrats."

Curtis put down his sandwich. "Hey, I may not have liked Bladen or even that local sheriff guy, but I had nothing to do with Bladen's demise. I can't say I didn't fantasize about it a few times, though." Curtis took another gulp of beer. “You and that Mark Twain person had a point about getting on with my life. So I did it. I was with someone when Bladen got shot, not that I can tell you who. I finally got a hold of my lawyer, your mamma, and she said I need to look like the wronged party so Ms. Hot-to-Trot looks like she’s the guilty party out to fleece me. I need to be the innocent victim in all this.”

Curtis picked up his sandwich and studied it. “Ya know,” he said in a thoughtful voice, “they say stuff happens for a reason and I believe the reason I got dumped was to find true love with someone who’s been though the same thing I have.”

Curtis got a dreamy look in his eyes. “I was walking through town and she was buying all these baskets and needed help hauling them. I offered and we got talking how she was doing this for the money and that she hated the guy paying her and then we got to laughing about all the things we had in common and... Well, things sort of progressed from there. It was love at first sight if you believe in such things and I sure do now.” Curtis puffed out his chest and bit into the sandwich. "You're looking at a lucky man," he said around lobster and mayo.

"And I'm sure Eileen feels the same way about you." I swiped another onion ring as Curtis sloshed beer all over the table. "And," Fiona continued, "just maybe as you and Eileen were talking, you both realized not only did you know the same people but you had it in for them. Then you set up this great plan to knock off Bladen and frame Sutter? Sounds like the perfect ending to a bad experience and I'm sure the police will think so too."

"Now wait just a minute." Curtis fisted his hands on the table.

"You took the pistol out of my shop." I nodded to drive home the point. "You were there, you had to see it. Eileen's been on the island for years and her father was a reenactor, so she knows the fort and muskets and drill schedules."

"You...you think my precious Eileen and I... That's ridiculous. That other wedding planner Petal or whatever her name is ran by us together in the guardhouse when

Bladen bought the farm and Eileen and I weren't exactly holding hands at the time. I paid Petal off to keep her yap shut 'cause of my Katie problems. She's one of those who'd do anything for a buck and if you two say anything about Eileen and me and this murder, I'll sue. Now get out of here and stay away from Eileen."

"Dang, I thought we had this all tied up," Fiona said when we left the Seabiscuit. We zipped our jackets against the drizzling fog as a gust whipped off the lake and chased leaves across Main Street. "We were really good back there."

"Except we were wrong. We accused an innocent guy and his new love of murder, and I don't have a clue where to go now. Look, it's getting late and even rotten overbearing cops from Detroit sleep. Maybe you should check on Finn. Maybe pick up a pizza at Island Slice and a six pack and try to salvage something from this rotten night."

"And," Fiona said, when we stopped in front of Mighty Mac Hamburgers, the scent of grilled cow and fries reminding me that I was starved. "You're not going off and doing something stupid on your own? Remember the hair and teeth."

"Maybe I'll write an apology letter."

"We'll send flowers. We're not going to get it right all the time, you know, but something will give. It's like Finn says, you got to trust the system."

"The only way I'm going to trust the system is when I see Sutter sitting behind his desk at the police station and Abrams getting on a ferry and heading back where he came from. Tell Finn I said hey."

I watched Fiona skip down Main Street. I headed for the bike shop as a flash of lightning cracked out over the lake. Sutter would be gone by now, and the kits would be watching *Animal Planet*. Sitting around waiting for Abrams to show up with a warrant was as appealing as a trip to the dentist.

Picking up the pace to outrun the rain, I headed for the Blarney Scone. Not that it would be open at this hour, but Irish Donna would be making scones for tomorrow.

The ultimate comfort food came from her oven and I was in desperate need of comfort.

"Blessed be the saints, what are you doing here at this hour and with a storm hot on your heels?" Irish Donna wiped her hands on her shamrock print apron smeared with stuff that makes up all things yummy. She closed the door behind me as another lightning strike hit closer and rattled the windows. I didn't realize how tired I was until the warmth of the little kitchen with white ruffled curtains at the windows and green and pink walls seeped into my bones.

Smells of butter, flour, and vanilla filled the air and golden brown puffs of blueberry-lemon, mocha, cranberry-orange, classic cream, and bacon-cheddar scones lined long, stainless steel cooling racks.

"If I get to heaven it'll look just like this," I said to Donna and meant every word. Fat raindrops smacked the windows and I parked myself on one of the stools at the cooling counter, feeling better than I had all day.

"And there ye go with the flattery. That must be meaning you need something? Tea and a nice scone do the trick, will it?"

"Tea and a scone would be salvation. Why so many scones tonight, not that I'm complaining. The world can't have too many scones."

"I'm putting that on the side of my buggy and riding it around town," Donna said with a laugh. She lit the flame under the teakettle on the massive stove and set a blueberry-lemon scone in front of me knowing it was my fave. I wasn't up on the requirements needed for a person to be dubbed a saint but this had to be close.

"The baking is for a rush order I just got today," Saint Donna added while pulling another tray of golden pastries from the over. "Seems that Petula person is making a fine name for herself. The mahjong club planned a small convention here on the island and that Bladen person didn't do a blessed thing about the opening breakfast at the butterfly house like he should. I don't know what the man could have been thinking."

Rain fell harder as Irish Donna slid her spatula under the scones and added them to the cooling racks. "But now Petula's paying me double and she's setting things to right. Going to make everyone happy."

Donna pulled off her oven mitts, poured tea, and handed me a business card. "Petula had these done up using the printer over at the library and they turned out nice. I like the little cake and champagne bottle in the corner. She's on the ball, that one is. No grass growing under her feet. I think she intends to make a go of it here on the island."

I sipped the tea. "Says on the card that she has a hospitality degree from Henry Ford College? That's in Detroit."

Donna sifted flour into a mixing bowl. "I suppose. That's where Henry be making his cars."

"Of course," I said talking to myself now more than Irish Donna. "Petula was from Detroit too. She worked for Bladen there and she had to know John. And she had to know Sutter and she was probably part of the gang. She had to be part of the undercover operation."

"Who's having an operation, dear?" Donna asked over the whirl of the electric mixer.

"It all fits. Sutter was the scapegoat while she had the money all along. She probably started the rumor that he took the money to take any suspicion off herself. She always flew under the radar, a hard worker and a little ditzy. She dressed like a bag lady so no one would suspect she had five million-"

"Five million dollars?" Irish Donna stopped the mixer, grabbed the gold shamrock around her neck, and stared at me. "Mercy be, now who be having that kind of money around these parts." Donna shook her head and cranked up the mixer.

"It's the perfect cover." I pointed to the little champagne bottle on the card. "Petula was at the fort, she ran by Curtis and Eileen so she was running from where? Knocking off Bladen maybe? And she knows the island and the Detroit area. She knows everything and everyone and she's been here all along. How could I be so blind? How could I be so stupid!"

Chapter Fourteen

"She's the brains behind the whole operation." I bit into a blueberry-lemon scone. "It's perfect."

"Why thank ye, dear." Irish Donna beamed.

"She's probably been spearheading the whole smuggling thing all along in Detroit then here on the island. Bladen had no idea."

I turned to Donna and yelled over the whirl of the mixer. "Do you know who rented Bladen Powers' barn space? It's probably on the east side of the island and not too far from the freight dock."

Irish Donna gave a final stir of chocolate chips into the batter with a big wooden spoon. "And I take it this barn might have something to do with all that stuff you've been babbling on about? Well, now that barn just might be up there at Overlook Cottage on Huron Road. Huron runs along behind the fort. It's the Linder place and Helen's having herself a fit that Frank's gone to renting out rooms in their Victorian trying to keep up with taxes that are getting to be a king's ransom these days. Frank's using that Airbnb you hear so much about. He rented the barn to Bladen to store wedding paraphernalia, but something's a bit off if ye asking me."

Donna dropped dollops of batter on cookie sheets. "At bingo on Tuesday Helen said she tried to take a little peek around the barn just to see what's what, but she couldn't get in. The locks were changed, do you believe, and there was newspaper taped over the windows so you couldn't see in. She thought there might be some hoochy-coochy going on, with Bladen being the Mr. Studly about town. Frank said Bladen was paying his rent on time and if the man was running a house of ill repute, it was none of his concern or hers and Helen should mind her own business. 'cept Helen was never one for that."

"No one on the island is one for that." I finished off my scone.

"And a good thing it is too. We'd all die of boredom, and I suppose you be heading up there tonight to see about this barn?" Donna pursed her lips.

"In this rain? Hardly, I'm not sure I could even find the place. There's nothing that can't wait 'til tomorrow." I downed the last of my tea.

"Meaning there's no stopping you."

"And you are not to follow me or call Mother or Fiona or anyone else if you ever want me to help serve wedding cake again."

"Considering how that last wedding cake event turned out, I'll be taking that as a promise more than a threat, me dear girl."

Irish Donna put down the spoon, snagged a flashlight from the shelf over the sink, and plucked a raincoat from the hook by the door. She handed both to me. "To be finding the barn, look for an old feed wagon they've done piled with yellow and purple mums as some fall decorations. It marks the driveway, but you need to look hard or you'll walk right by it and... Oh, for Pete's Sake."

Donna turned off the oven, untied her apron and flung it over a stool, and grabbed another flashlight. “I best be coming with you as ye will never find the place in this downpour. And another thing is that Nate’s a great chap and the only way you two will ever get together is if you don’t up and die on me. Going snooping like this just might make it happen.”

Donna put the sheet of scones in the fridge to bake later and snagged another rain slicker as a crack of lightning electrified the sky. We made for the door.

“The good thing is,” Donna said as we hurried along with rain dripping off our raincoats’ hoods. “Nobody with the sense God gave little green apples will be out in this here mess.”

“Unless they’re building an ark.”

“Don’t be tempting fate now. Never good to be tempting fate with a killer on the loose.”

We trudged down Market Street, rivulets of water snaking across our path. Puddles pooled everywhere and streetlights and shop lights blended into swirls of color on the wet pavement. Diehard barflies darted from one watering hole to the other as Donna and I scrunched up into our raincoats with me trying to ignore how my gym shoes were soaked clear through.

We started up Fort Street as cascades of water rushed towards us, giving me new respect for spawning salmon. It also gave me more respect for Irish Donna who had at least thirty years and thirty pounds on me. We huddled close to the shops to cut the wind, the only sounds the moan of foghorns and the split splat of our footsteps until we got to the top of the hill. The white walls of Fort Mackinac loomed to the right, the Governor's House to the left, and the lights of the town glistened below. I followed Irish Donna onto Huron Street.

"Least we be out of the wind now." Donna clicked on her flashlight and I did the same.

"I think the worse of the storm's over, at least for a bit." I looked up to a star sneaking out from behind the clouds as we rounded a bend. Overlook Cottage, which was more Daddy Warbucks than Winnie the Pooh, sat to one side and Irish Donna pointed to the flower wagon up ahead.

"Here is the lane. Bless be, we made it and I wasn't all that sure we would with it raining cats and dogs. We need to be turning off the flashlights so we don't look like we're leading a parade. You can make out the house just ahead with the lights a blazing. Helen used to have us all to her place for Christmas brunch, but that was before she got bad arthritis in her knees and Frank turned into a big old tightwad. The barn's around back if I remember right."

Irish Donna looked at me her eyes bright even in the darkness. "So now what, me dear?"

"You're enjoying this, aren't you?"

"There's only so much flour and butter a woman can take in one night before she goes a little loopy in the head."

Using the light from the house to navigate, we made our way down the lane, trying to avoid puddles and mud, not that my shoes could get much dirtier. Gravel crunched underfoot, more stars popped out overhead, and the night was ink black since no moon follows a full moon.

Ducking down, we scooted below a big bay window and skirted around a fountain with a woman pouring water out of a jug. We wedged ourselves against the apple trees so we could stay off the beaten path and out of sight.

"I think the barn door be on the far side," Irish Donna whispered as we both stumbled over a log and nearly landed on our faces. "And why is there a motor running of all things?"

"Air conditioning." With the rain slowing to a drizzle, I slid back the hood of my raincoat and Donna did the same. "Bladen stores wine for weddings and events so he needed the AC for temperature control and a place that could accommodate drays and deliveries. Sure hope there's not an alarm system."

"It's an old barn on Mackinac Island, not the Federal Reserve." We slogged up to what I hoped was the barn and I undid the purple paperclips from my jacket.

"I'll go inside and you stay out here," I said to Irish Donna. "If things blow up you'll have to call in the Calvary. Petula's already knocked off two guys and gotten away with it and nobody knows we're here. We don't need the body count to jump to four."

Donna parked her hand on her hip, flipped back her red curls, and stuck out her bottom lip. "I came all this here way through rain and storm and gloom of night to stand out in the dark like an old fencepost?"

"You came all this way to one-up Mildred Fernwright's gossip when you get your hair done at Village Glam.

But for now, put your hand over the flashlight to cut the brightness and aim at the lock so I can see."

"How'd you learn how to do this?" Donna asked as I straightened the clips.

"The same way you know how to bake the world's best scones." I hunched down to get a better view of the lock and jabbed in one paperclip then the other, hoping I wasn't working on one of those super fancy Yale gizmos. "Practice, practice, practice."

I twisted one of the prongs, kept one in place, and felt the pins give way. The main cylinder turned then turned a little more. I grabbed the knob and slid back the door. "Tada!"

"My word and williwigs! Ye went and did it."

"Don't tell Mother, it'll just give her something else to worry about. If Petula shows up, knock three times on the barn door so I can hide."

"And if she does show up, how do you plan on getting out?"

"I'm working on it."

Irish Donna slipped off the shamrock she wore around her neck and looped the gold chain over my head. "This isn't the first time you've given me your lucky charm," I said.

"And the way things are going around here, it won't be anywhere near the last." Irish Donna added a smile and I slipped inside the barn, pulling the door closed behind me. I reset the lock in case Petula showed up, so she wouldn't suspect someone was inside, and turned on the flashlight. I took a look around as the AC hummed in the background.

The barn was more of a mini warehouse than a barn. Boxes of tablecloths, napkins, aisle runners, and vases sat on one group of shelves. A pile of wicker flower stands was parked in the corner while plastic tubs of white candles, blue candles, cream pillars, spools of lace, tulle, and ribbon of every size and color imaginable filled another section of shelving. A bunch of empty boxes from Sandhill Crane Vineyards was heaped in a corner and a map of Lake Michigan and Huron was taped to the wall with the *Barefoot Gal's* schedules beside it.

Cases of Dom Perignon with its crest logo stamped on the outside were stacked in a row organized by vintage - 2004, 2005, 2009. Cases of Louis Roederer Cristol Brute 2009 with a gold oval logo were stacked next to the Dom and Champagne Armand de Brignac Brute. I recognized the Ace of Spades champagne logo from my parents' twenty-fifth wedding anniversary party. There were more cases of other champagnes that I didn't recognize, but since my areas of expertise were Nutty Buddies, buttercream icing, and Bud Lite, I was way out of my league.

So, we had wines and champagnes and a lot of wedding stuff, but none of it was illegal. It's what was needed to pull off a wedding. A really nice wedding, but again not criminal unless you were the father of the bride footing the bill for all this - I'm sure it seemed criminal to him. So what were Bladen and Petula up to that—

Three soft knocks echoed throughout the warehouse and I shoved my hand over the flashlight beam, leaving only enough light to find my way to the cases of Dom since that was the tallest stack. I wedged myself behind it as the door opened, lights came on, and I found myself toe-to-toe and chest-to chest with Nate Sutter. I got an exasperated *what the heck are you doing here* look and gave Sutter a *what the heck are you doing here* look of my own.

This wasn't so bad, except for the chest-to-chest thing that brought back images of Hello Kitty and beyond. Sutter and I could take Petula except take her for what? Being a wedding planner? But if she found Sutter, then that would really be bad, and—

Penny, knock, knock, knock, Penny, knock, knock, knock sounded from my back pocket and echoed like a brass band throughout the quiet barn. Really? Cell phone service *now*? I fumbled with my flashlight to get the phone out of my pocket while Sutter closed his eyes and shook his head and Petula stuck her head around the cases of Dom.

"Hello?" I said into the phone.

"Evie, is that really you?" came Fiona's voice. "The storm must have zapped something and we got service, isn't that totally cool. Anyway, you'll never guess what, Finn said he loves me."

"I'm a little busy here."

"Me! He loves me. He bought flowers and candy and good champagne not the cheap stuff from Doud's and he thinks Nate needs to make a run for it and we came up with a plan to make it happen. Abrams said the FBI is coming in tomorrow and they'll find Nate for sure and the evidence against him is just too damning. Have you seen Nate?"

"He's standing right here."

"Yeah, right. Sure he is. Meet Finn at the bike shop in twenty. Nothing's going to happen until tomorrow so the bike shop is safe until then and you need to find Nate right now."

I disconnected and slid Sheldon in my pocket. Petula looked from me to Sutter. "Hope I'm not interrupting."

There was a knock at the door and it slid back to, "Yoo-hoo, anybody home?" Irish Donna's footsteps came closer. "I'm sorry to be barging in like this but I was wondering if I could...uh...be borrowing a cup of sugar, I'm always running out of sugar, you see."

Petula folded her arms. "Let me guess, the Mackinac Island comedy hour?"

"I know you did it," I said to Petula. Sutter and I scooted from behind the champagne cases and Irish Donna pulled up beside me. "I know you knocked off Bladen and John and you're behind the whole smuggling operation in Detroit and here. You have the five million dollars that's gone missing and you can't knock off all three of us so you might as well confess everything and give up now."

Petula spread her arms wide. "Honey, you are downright delusional. Do I look like I have five million dollars? If I did I'd be on a beach in the Caribbean sipping something with an umbrella in it." Petula waved her hand over the wedding items. "Smuggling what?"

"This." Sutter picked up a case of Dom 2004, walked it over to the box with the Sandhill logo, and dropped the case of Dom neatly inside. Sutter closed the flaps and ran a strip of packing tape across the seam.

"You order extra champagne as part of weddings," Sutter said. "You pay for the extra yourself then ship it off to Canada under the Sandhill Wines logo. The wine distributors in Canada pick up their orders, pay the duty and taxes that is not much on cheap wine running ten buck a bottle. They wire transfer you funds and now they have champagne that's worth two-hundred-fifty, three-hundred, four-hundred bucks a bottle."

"I don't have the money and as for the rest..." Petula tossed her head. "Prove it. John and Bladen are dead so they're not talking and the guys in Canada are never going to give up this good deal. Who's going to listen to the ramblings of a crooked cop and the crazies trying to get him off the hook."

Petula nodded at Sutter. "Soon you'll be behind bars in Detroit and we all know what happens to cops in prison. You won't be talking much then. The only reason I'm not calling the cops myself is because the phones are screwed up. I didn't do in Bladen, you did because you have the money. You did me a favor." She waved her hand over the barn. "Now this is all mine. I'll lay low until you're tried and convicted so it looks like the smuggling ended with you, but then I'll start up again and it'll be business as usual."

"Someone will figure this all out, you just wait and see," Irish Donna insisted.

"In your dreams. Honey, they've had two years and came up with zip. With Mackinac Island being out of the way like it is and nothing but a bunch of fudge-eating tourists, it's not on anyone's radar."

Petula went to the door, yanked it open, and said to Nate, “If I were you, I’d take that five mil you stole and run. You’re never getting out of this. The evidence against you is too solid. You, Nate Sutter, are toast.”

Chapter Fifteen

"Running is the only way out," Finn said to Sutter, the three of us in the dark bike shop as rain beat steadily against the porch roof. I sat on the stool, Bambino and Cleveland took up space on the workbench, and Sutter paced the room.

"The FBI's coming in tomorrow on the first ferry." Finn sat on the other stool. "With your fingerprints on the gun, and everyone thinking you ran off with the money, that's motive and opportunity. Abrams thinks he's got this case sewed up."

Sutter raked back his wet hair. "Except I'm innocent."

"So Fiona and I cooked up this plan, Finn went on. "Fiona saw the *Barefoot Gal* crew in the Pink Pony. I bought them a round and told them I wanted to get off Fudge Island. Barefoot has two berths for passengers and in this weather you can slip onboard and hide in my room. Next stop from here is Sault Ste. Marie. The *Gal* is heading out tonight as soon as the storm blows over. You'll go ashore in Canada as John Bernard, coxswain, and get lost."

"Passport?" I asked, trying to come to grips with Sutter leaving. "He's not going anywhere without that and Nathaniel Sutter's picture is plastered all over the media by now."

Finn tossed the blue booklet onto the workbench. "Here you go thanks to Molly. You look enough like John Bernard to use his passport and John's a regular in Sault Ste. Marie. Customs won't give you a second glance and Canada won't have the official update that John's dead. It takes a week for that info to go international."

"You're taking a hell of a risk doing this for me."

Finn walked over to Sutter. "I got you into this undercover operation in the first place and I need to fix it. I know this means you're going to be on the run, but it's better than being in a prison cell."

Finn checked his watch. "We gotta move right now. The storm's letting up and the *Gal* will shove off in less than an hour. I left a note for Abrams saying I was taking vacation so I didn't have to be involved in the takedown of a friend. It'll be days before they realize you're gone too."

"But won't they connect the dots?" I asked Finn. "They'll know you helped Sutter escape and then your neck is on the chopping block."

"There're a lot of boats on these lakes, and who knows when Nate took off. He could have stolen away on a pleasure boat, on a ferry, on a plane headed out of here, done the backstroke to Saint Ignace for all they know. There's no connecting us, and Nate has a lot of friends that would help him escape. No reason to single me out. Look, I've got two years until early retirement. It'll give me time to get evidence against Petula. From what you and Nate said, she's the ringleader of all of this."

Sutter turned to Finn. "I'll follow in about ten minutes and leave by the back door. I can cut through the trees and around Mission Point to the dock. I'll wait by the warehouse. Signal me aboard when the coast is clear."

"With both of us in dark raingear and hoods the crew will think I'm you." Finn flashed me a tight smile. "Thanks for the help, Evie. This isn't over by a long shot. See you around." Finn flipped up the hood on his windbreaker and closed the front door behind him. His footsteps clattered across the wood planks of the porch until his silhouette faded into the rain.

I pulled the green paint can aka cash register from under the workbench, pulled off the lid, and wadded up the bills inside. I thrust them at Sutter. "You'll need this."

"I'm not taking your money."

"Yeah, like what are you going to do, use the ATM so Abrams and his merry men know exactly where you are? They have a bead on all your accounts, that's the first thing they do, follow the money." I opened Sutter's hand and smooshed the wadded money into his palm. "You can pay me when you get back."

Our gaze fused through the dark as we both thought *if you get back*. "Take care of Mom and Rudy," Sutter said in a tight voice. He let out a deep breath then slammed his fisted hand on the workbench. "This is total crap. I'm a cop. I uphold the law. I don't break it."

"I'll keep an eye on Petula and get Captain and the guys at the docks to watch if she makes a move. We'll get her."

"Unless she changes locations, wine boxes, ports, deliveries to Canada. She'll mix it up like they did in Detroit. Nobody will know what to look for and even if Petula does get caught smuggling, that's not the two murders. Nothing links her to those, that's all on me. She's smart, a whole lot smarter than I thought, to pull this off."

"Yeah, well...well I'm smart too." I had to say something so I wouldn't cry.

Sutter gave me a half smile. "Yeah, you are that." He slid his arm around my waist, pulled me close, and kissed me like there was no tomorrow. "Bye, Chicago," he whispered. "Remember that I love you."

Then Nate Sutter headed for the door to the kitchen and closed it behind him.

"What? No! Wait!" The outside back door clicked shut and I turned to the kits. "Do something."

Bambino and Cleveland looked as forlorn as I felt. "What the heck? Who says I love you and leaves? What am I supposed to do now?"

"I know what I'm going to do," Fiona sing-songed as she burst through the front door with the last of the thunder rumbling across the sky. She shook the rain from her navy windbreaker with a red streak and collapsed her umbrella. She dropped it on the floor and tangoed my way, leaving raindrops in her wake. "I've decided to go with Finn and Nate on *Barefoot Gal*. Isn't that the best idea ever?"

She toed the suitcase she'd dragged in behind her. "I'll be the perfect cover for Nate. Finn and I will be together looking like we're on a romantic getaway and when the ferry leaves Sault Ste. Marie and Nate's safely away in Canada, Finn and I will stay on the ferry until it gets to Detroit and ooh-la-la."

"It's a working ferry, not the Queen Mary, and this isn't a ooh-la-la romantic rendezvous, Fiona. In case you forgot, Nate's life is on the line."

"I haven't forgotten. You'll find the killer, you always do. My great romantic ferry plan makes Finn's trip look spontaneous. It's more like Finn and I couldn't wait to be off together and it takes Nate's escape completely out of the equation. Finn forgot his jacket and I thought I'd bring it to him when I visited next month, but I thought why not just take it to him now on the ferry. Then again, why not just stay on the ferry. Brilliant, huh? I packed champagne and a sexy nightie."

Fiona flashed me an impish grin. "All I need now is for you to water my plants. Are you listening to me at all, Evie?"

"Sure." *Maybe.*

Fiona pulled a key from her purse then took a string from pocket. "I'm tying my house key to this screwdriver with the red handle that's here on your workbench so when you screw something you'll remember to water my ficus. Got it?"

"What's a ficus?"

"Green leafy thing in the hall that will curse you forever if you don't water it."

Fiona flung her purse over her shoulder as Cal rolled in the front door. "Finally," he said shoving back the hood of his windbreaker. "I've been trying to call you all night to see what's going on with Nate and the phones are down because of the storm. Why are you two sitting in the dark and what's with the suitcase?"

"Evie'll fill you in. I have a boat to catch." Fiona handed Cal the screwdriver and kissed him on the cheek. "Water my plants, okay? Miss Marple's brain is in whodunit land and she's not going to remember a blasted thing I said."

Fiona grabbed her suitcase and umbrella and pointed at the door. "Watch out, Canada, here I come. I'll send postcards and bring back syrup." She laughed and ran out.

"Fiona's going to Canada in the middle of the night?" Cal stared at the door. "I'm not going to like your answer, am I?"

"Finn's smuggling Sutter onto the *Barefoot Gal* and then into Canada and Fiona's along for the ride and I need a Nutty Buddy fix real quick."

"Smuggling Nate?" Cal and the kits followed me to the kitchen. "Oh, good. What can go wrong with that plan."

I flipped on the lights to the last raindrops splatting against the back window. I headed for the fridge. "I can't come up with a better plan and with all the evidence against Sutter, what else is there to do? You know he won't last a week in jail."

I handed Cal a beer, gave the kits sitting on the windowsill Fancy Feast treats, and pulled a Nutty Buddy from the freezer. "My stupid black cloud keeps getting bigger and bigger."

"And the woman I love is headed off with another guy and I get to water her plants. It's a great day for both of us." Cal clinked his beer bottle to my Nutty Buddy and I snagged the screwdriver from his hand.

"I'll do the watering. If you go to Fiona's," I said around a melting mouthful that usually tasted wonderful and tonight smacked of wallpaper paste. "You'll mope."

"Marines do not mope. Well, maybe a little when no one's looking."

I stared at the screwdriver and the silver key dangling off the end. "Fiona's a Wonder Woman kind of girl or maybe Catwoman or Cher if she's feeling frisky. She hates Hello Kitty." I took another bite of ice cream and started to feel a little sick. "Why did she use a Hello Kitty ribbon to tie her key to the screwdriver?"

"Is this a trick question?"

"Maybe. I mean why did she even have it, I can't see her buying Hello Kitty ribbon and... I know this ribbon. Look right there."

I used the tip of my ice cream cone to point to a spot. "It's a yellow lube stain, Teflon C130 for bikes. It's got that icky green tint to it that looks like snot. Anyway, I keep it on my workbench 'cause I'm always greasing up the bike chains. The last time I saw this ribbon it was tied around that pistol award box that Nate got. The glass lid kept sliding off," I said as much to myself as Cal, trying to remember exactly what happened. "I tied the lid on with the ribbon so the glass wouldn't break and I got the ribbon off the Hello Kitty kite up there," I pointed to the ceiling, "when I unpacked it from the delivery box and-"

"Waitaminute. Holdon. The ribbon was tied around the pistol that shot Bladen?" Cal set the Bud on the table. "Are you sure?"

"I kept the box on my workbench and when it was gone I figured Sutter or Molly took it but then they found the pistol wadded up in the material at the fort. So how did this ribbon get in Fiona's pocket?"

My heart dropped into my stomach, my Nutty Buddy dripping all over my hand and onto the floor. "It's not Fiona's pocket. That jacket Fiona had on isn't hers. It's Finn's. It had the red paint streak across the front that I put there. He forgot the jacket at her house."

"Finn took the award box? Finn took the pistol?"

I tossed the ice cream in the sink and grabbed a towel. “He was in Detroit, he was here, he was at the fort. He knows guns and he knew Bladen and John and Sutter. He spearheaded the undercover operation, all the details of the takedown in Detroit, where the cops were looking next, so he could ship out the smuggled booze to another port.”

“But why kill John and Bladen? They were his guys. They worked for him.”

“Except they didn’t know that.”

Cal’s eyes widened. “He did it to frame Nate for the murders.”

“And frame him for taking the money. Then Finn could walk off with it free and clear. He’s got the loot stashed in some offshore bank account and he started the rumor that Sutter was here on the island so John and Bladen would find him. Finn showing up was a great cover, romancing Fiona made him one of us and none of us suspected a blasted thing. How could we be so totally stupid?”

I turned to Bambino and Cleveland. “They knew what was going on. They never trusted Finn, never sucked up to him like they do to the rest of you. No purrs, no lap-sitting.”

“And now Finn’s going to dump Fiona and Nate in the lake. With all that money, he has enough to pay off the captain and crew to look the other way. Or he’ll say Sutter and Fiona never got on board in the first place and ran off together.”

“The phones are down. I have to get to the ferry before it leaves port.”

“And do what?”

“What would a Marine do?”

“Have enough firepower to take over a small country.”

“Other than that.”

“Diversion. Stall. I’ll come up with something on this end. Go!”

Chapter Sixteen

I pushed Firefly out onto the front porch as the last trickles of rain dribbled off the shop roof and splashed onto Main Street. I grabbed the gold shamrock around my neck and held it tight. “Okay, I can do this,” I said out loud to myself. “Get on bike, stay on bike. For a change, a big change, do not fall off bike.”

“Darling daughter, you can’t stay on a bike in broad daylight with the sun shining.” Dressed head to toe in badass black, Mother walked up beside me pushing the really sweet road bike Angelo gave her for Christmas.

“Where are you going?”

“With you, of course. Cal came over and gave me the ten-cent version of what’s going on and threw in something about needing a diversion. Since I probably can’t talk you out of going after Nate, I’m here to divert.”

"Not a good idea. You could get hurt and if that happens Angelo will hunt me down."

"Bloomfields do not get hurt, we do the hurting if any needs to be done. Now let's go, we're wasting time." Mother pedaled off as if she'd been born on a bike. I took a deep breath, let go of the shamrock, and pushed off, waddling my way down the street behind her

"Temperature's dropping," Mother called over her shoulder. "Looks like fog is replacing the rain. We have low clouds overhead and a nice mist covering the pavement."

"I can't see the road."

"And the bad guys won't be able to see us. Well, not all that well. Just follow me and you'll be fine."

"Your lips to God's ears," I mumbled to myself as Mother pulled ahead. She neatly dodged a puddle the size of a small pond, and I zigged and zagged and ran straight through the puddle, splashing water everywhere and getting totally soaked.

"Are you okay back there?"

"Just ducky." Considering my drenched state, the duck reference was very accurate and I was still upright. The age of miracles was not dead.

Mother's headlight ahead of me and Round Island lighthouse flashing every ten seconds to the right kept me oriented. I played connect the dots, riding from one hazy cone of streetlight to the next all the way to Mission Point Resort. Mother and I rounded the last bend, leaving the resort lights behind, the two of us now cocooned in total darkness between the inky black lake and high cliffs.

"The turn-off's here," I called to Mother. Good news is that the lane was before Lake Shore turned into Mount Everest. The bad news was that I had no rescue plan and wet gravel slid me headfirst into a tree.

"Evie, say something." Mother peered down at me.

"I want my Honda Civic."

The stench of diesel fuel saturated the damp air and I pointed to the ghostly-gray fluorescents illuminating the dock. "That's *Barefoot Gal* at the end of the dock. We'll go the rest of way on foot." I pulled Sheldon from my pocket. "We'll use one light so they don't see us coming."

Keeping to the weedy bushes on the right, we slogged our way through the mud to the warehouse. "The crew's untying the mooring lines." Mother nodded up ahead. "The engines are powering up. They're getting ready to shove off."

"Stay here. I've got an idea." I crept across the gravel lane and made my way up the dock, darting between the recycling crates lining the pier. Angry lake waves larger than usual from the storm splashed over the dock and incoming fog twisted around my ankles. I headed for the rope that the deckhand had already untied and when he got busy untying another line from a piling, I grabbed the freed rope to retie it. Except I couldn't lift it and retie at the same time because the stupid rain-soaked rope weighed a ton and I'd been eating Nutty Buddies when I should have been going to the gym. I tried again and this time hoisting the rope was much easier due to the fact that Mother was on the other side lifting with me.

"I said to stay put."

"And where's the fun in that? Besides, no one tells Bloomfield women what to do, even other Bloomfield women." Mother flashed me a big smile and together we looped the rope over the big fat wood piling.

"Now *Barefoot Gal* isn't going anywhere." Mother gave the rope an extra pat. "Unless she takes the whole dock with her. I think that counts as a diversion, don't you. Let's go find your boyfriend."

"He's not my boyfriend, though he did say he loved me." I needed to tell someone.

"And you need to remember that, dear." Mother clam-crawled up the metal gangplank while the deckhand undid the last rope at the back of the boat. I followed, our footfalls being drowned out by the rumble of the big engines revving for takeoff. We passed a stairway to the left and hid behind a recycling crate as the deckhand clambered up the gangplank. He paused by the railing and pushed a button. The gangplank started to rise.

"Staterooms are on the deck below," Mother whispered as the guy headed to the back of the boat, "a little something I picked up on that Caribbean cruise with Angelo last February. Have any idea what to do when we find Nate?"

"Hit Finn over the head with one of the champagne bottles that Fiona brought along and run like hell?"

"That'll work."

Together Mother and I peeked out from behind the crate. "You lower the gangplank so we can get off this tub," Mother said. "I'll find the stateroom."

Mother tippy-toed her way to the stairs as I edged my way over to the railing. The button marked *Lower* was a good bet so I pressed it. The gangplank stopped, then reversed. I made my way to the steps and stopped dead as I heard a gruff voice below say, "Hey, lady, what are you doing here?"

"Selling Avon. Can I interest you in a new lotion or aftershave."

"Save it for the captain."

"Is he an Avon man?"

"He's an angry man. Get moving."

Great! Now the bad guys had Mother. And they had Nate and Fiona! Where were the Marines? Weren't they supposed to be landing about now with all that firepower? What to do? I had no idea what to do! I checked out the stairs, made sure no one else was there, and started down. Should I go after Mother or stick with the original plan? With whacking Finn as my *only* plan I went with that.

Doors marked *Storage, Crew Quarters,* and *State Room 201* lined the outside walkway. I kept below the line of sight of the window in Stateroom 201 and put my ear to the door. I heard Nate's voice and was that Fiona's giggle? Finn had tricked her, played her like a well-tuned violin and would break her heart. And that's if we got out of this mess alive.

I stuck the paperclips in the lock, and fiddled with the pins. The lock flipped, the revving engines strained against the rope holding *Barefoot Gal* in place, and I eased open the door. Crawling inside I hunkered down behind a leather club chair next to Finn's duffle and Fiona's suitcase.

It wasn't the Ritz, not that I'd ever been to the Ritz, but the stateroom had two queen beds, a nice sofa, and two club chairs with Sutter in the one across the room.

"It's going to work out fine," Finn was saying to Sutter. Finn was on the couch while Fiona was sitting on the bed thumbing through what I imagined was *Young Bride* magazine. Sutter spied me, nearly dropping the glass in his hand, and I gave him a little finger wave.

"It's a good plan." Sutter said not looking one bit glad to see me. "With all the evidence the FBI would have me behind bars for life that wouldn't be all that long."

I pointed to Finn and made a gun with my thumb and forefinger and mouthed *killer*. Then I put my hands around my throat as if strangling myself and stuck out my tongue and crossed my eyes like I was dying, hoping that Sutter would take my fine acting ability to mean *Let's get Finn 'cause he's the bad guy*.

Finn continued on about what Sutter would do in Canada and Sutter stared at me for what seemed like an eternity. He shook his head *no*. I bobbed my head *yes* and

Sutter shook another *no*. What was wrong with that man! My mother was in the hands of bad dudes, he and Fiona were about to be fish food, and I would be dessert. Finn crossed the room and turned around and I saw the gun stuck in his waistband. Oh, that's why Sutter was saying no.

The engines revved harder and any minute now the crew would realize what was going on with the ropes and all hope of escape would be over. I needed that diversion.Jumping up and yelling *surprise* didn't smack of a good idea so I went with the champagne plan. Finn was too far away for me to run up behind him and clobber him before he clobbered me or I got his gun. But there were other things I could do with champagne. Reaching inside Fiona's suitcase I felt around and slid out a champagne bottle. I held it up for Sutter to see and got another *no* headshake coupled with a steely look. But, like Mother said, no one tells Bloomfield women what to do.

I shook the bottle hard, twisted off the little wire cage at the top holding the cork in place, prided up the cork just a tiny bit and--

"Pow!"

Finn spun around then reached for his gun. In that split second Sutter made a grab for the gun but wasn't fast enough. Finn pointed the gun at me and Sutter stopped dead and backed away. "I knew you were trouble," Finn hissed.

"And I should have known you were scum."

"What? Who? Eviewhyareyouhere?" Fiona jumped off the bed and faced Finn. "Why are you pointing a gun at Evie?"

"Get over there by Nate," Finn said to me, his blue eyes now cold and calculating. He turned to Fiona. "You too, cupcake."

"Finn's the killer," I said to Fiona.

"No. That's impossible. He was here to save Nate." Fiona shook her head hard.

"Not exactly." I took Fiona's hand and pulled her beside me. "He set Sutter up from the beginning. He framed Sutter for the two murders and he's the one who ran off with five million dollars. Cops like money too."

"But...but you like me." Fiona stared at Finn. "You...you love me, you said so. I'm your girl. I'm your sunshine."

Sutter put his arm around Fiona. "I'm sorry."

The door burst open with Abrams framed in the doorway and Molly right behind him.

"Perfect timing." Finn said to Abrams in official cop voice. "Good that you're here. I tracked Nate to the boat and caught him trying to escape. No matter how good of friends we are I couldn't let that happen. These two," Finn nodded at Fiona and me, "were smuggling him into Canada."

"What?" I gasped.

"This was your plan!" Fiona yelled at Finn. "Yours and mine. We ate pizza, drank beer, fooled around. You booked this room in your name so Nate could get away."

Finn did the innocent shoulder-roll routine. "Nice try, Fiona. I know you grew up with Nate so I don't really blame you for trying to save him. I blame Nate for being a crook and killer and getting you involved. The room is booked in your name."

"It's a lie." I faced Abrams. "It's all lies. Finn is the one who stole all the money in Detroit, he's the head honcho who set up the smuggling there, and he killed John and Bladen. He's framing Nate for the murders and for taking the money and he's framing Fiona and me right now. You've got to see that!"

"Nate's your friend," Abrams said to Finn. "You can holster your gun. I can take it from here. I got this covered."

Finn gave me a smirky grin then stuck his gun in his back holster and Abrams said to Molly. "Cuff him."

"No, no, no! You got this all wrong!" I jumped in front of Sutter. Abrams pulled me back and Molly took out her handcuffs and headed for Sutter. Then she did a quick sidestep and quickly slapped the handcuffs on an unsuspecting Finn.

"Finn McCabe," Abrams said. "You are under arrest for the murders of John Bernard and Bladen Powers and for international smuggling, racketeering, money laundering, and-"

"And lying to me, you big fat rotten jerk!" Fiona yelled as she lunged for Finn, beating him on the chest with her fists and kicking him in the shins and was that a knee to where no knee should be?

"Get her off of me," Finn yelped as he hunched over in pain, with Fiona now pounding her fists on his back. "Get her off! I want a lawyer."

Abrams shoved a hunched over Finn into a club chair and flashed me an FBI badge. "We suspected Finn was behind the smuggling operation all along but couldn't prove anything. Then Nate contacted us when he found John dead on the dock and we set things in motion. We never figured he'd go after Bladen but I think Bladen was on to Finn so he had to go too. Finn's framing of Nate was flawless."

"He's a cop, one of the best I've ever known. He taught me a lot." Sutter puffed out a sigh. "He knew all the tricks and he knew not to touch the five million. But then he needed to pay off the boat captain and the crew. We figured sooner or later he'd have to pay off someone."

"We traced the wire transfer he made tonight and we nailed him."

"But you won't get him for murder?" Fiona asked. "I want him to hang, blast it all."

"John cut his attacker with a box cutter that we have and my guess is Finn here has a fresh cut somewhere."

"His side!" Fiona jabbed her finger at Finn and snarled, "I saw it with my own two eyes." She swiped up the *Young Bride* magazine and flung it at Finn. "So there, you no good, two-timing jackass."

"Mother!" I gasped. "The captain has her."

"After explaining the difference between smuggling a few cases of champagne and getting involved in murder, Carman's probably beating the pants off him in a game of poker while we take care of things here," Sutter added all calm and cool and relaxed. Actually, the man was more relaxed than I'd seen him... ever.

"Mother knew? My very own mother was in on this?"

Molly nodded. "Nate needed a confidant on the island. Someone with a clear head which left me out."

I held my arms wide. "What am I, chopped liver?"

"Girlfriend, what you are is a terrible liar," Fiona said.

I glared at Sutter. "One little word is all I needed from you." I walked toward Sutter backing him across the cabin. "Just one word that this was all going to end well. I worried about you. My cats worried about you."

I poked Sutter in the chest. "I lost sleep, chewed my fingernails. I got wrinkles and I do not need wrinkles at my age."

Sutter took me by the shoulders. "To pull this off we needed you in black cloud mode. We needed you to be Evie Bloomfield, the woman on a mission who never gives up no matter the odds. You had to be one hundred percent believable when everything was going wrong or Finn would have never believed that he was getting away with it. He would have smelled a rat."

"You're the rat!"

Sutter held me a little tighter, his eyes soft and warm, a smile on his face. "We could never have gotten Finn without you. I told you to remember that I love you and I do, I really do. You're the very best thing that's ever happened to me, Chicago. It might take some time but can you forgive me?"

"How much time do you have?" I grumped.

Sutter grinned, a devilish glint in his dark eyes. He wrapped his arms around me. "There's a long cold winter ahead of us, Chicago. I bet we can figure something out."

CPSIA information can be obtained
at www.ICGtesting.com
Printed in the USA
LVHW020322160622
721378LV00003B/242

9 781729 374788